# NAILING THE ALIEN

## BEASTLY ALIEN BOSS, BOOK 1

## AVA ROSS

NAILING THE ALIEN

Beastly Alien Boss Series, Book 1

Copyright © 2022 Ava Ross

Cover art by Natasha Snow Designs

Editing/Proofreading by Owl Eyes Proofs & Edits & Del's Diabolical
Editing

AISN: B0B113JTV7

❀ Created with Vellum

# FOREWORD

A note to the reader.

If you found this book outside of Amazon,
it's likely a stolen/pirated copy.
Authors make nothing when books are pirated.
If authors are not paid for their work,
they can't afford to keep writing.

*For my mom who*
*always believed in me.*

*And for Dad.*
*I found your handwritten stories*
*among your things!*
*They're amazing.*

# BOOKS BY AVA

## MAIL-ORDER BRIDES OF CRAKAIR

Vork

Bryk

Jorg

Kral

Wulf

Lyel

Axil, Gaje

(Companion novellas)

---

## BRIDES OF DRIEGON

Malac

Drace

Rashe

Teran

Kruze, Allor, Skoar

(Companion novellas)

Alien Warrior Untamed

Alien Warrior Unbeaten

Alien Warrior Unclaimed

---

## ALIEN WARRIOR ABANDONED/

## SHATTERED GALAXIES

Ravaged World

Ravaged Realm

---

BEASTLY ALIEN BOSS

Nailing the Alien

Leashing the Alien

Catering to the Alien

Cultivating the Alien

Escorting the Alien

(A Companion Novella)

You can find my books on Amazon.

# NAILING THE ALIEN

**My short-term construction job with a
beastly orc boss just got complicated.**

Desperate to escape the clutches of the alien lizard mafia,
I accept a spur-of-the-moment job offer on a distant
planet. A monstrous, grumpy alien orc is building a new
home in a distant colony, and he's looking for an
assistant.

He needs me to hold his hammer. I get it. It's a big
hammer.

He's a lonely barbarian brute with a gruff exterior, but I
soon learn that inside he's hiding a squishy center. When
he unexpectedly enters his mating frenzy, there's no one
around to handle the job . . . except me. He gives me two
options—return home or stay and help him with a whole
different kind of nailing . . .

*Nailing the Alien* is Book 1 in the Beastly Alien Boss Series. Each features a rough and ready alien who can't resist falling for his fated mate.

# 1

## CORA

I raced through the street with three Vessars snapping at my heels. My sneakers slammed on the cracked concrete, and I barely avoided placing my foot in something dead, flat, and slimy.

This was my damn cousin's fault. If he were around, I'd load him in a rocket launcher and shoot him all the way to the Dundire Quadrant.

He bailed from Earth three days ago, taking a one-way shuttle to who knows where, leaving me to clean up his mess. His mess being a sizeable debt owed to the Vessar alien lizard mafia.

They seemed to think they could collect it from me. Haha. I didn't even have enough credits to buy a cup of juva. And if I showed up on my mom's stoop to beg, she'd slam the door in my face. We got along best when we didn't talk or see each other.

As for my dad, I wasn't sure who he was, and Mom wasn't telling.

The Vessars growled, their breath hot on the back of my neck.

"No problem," the Vessar boss had said. "You can paysss hisss debt wit youself. I sellsss to someone decent. Promise."

Like I believed his promise?

No can do, dudes. I liked my simple life, and I planned to keep it auction-free. A sale meant slavery to an alien for the rest of my days.

A Vessar's suction-cupped limb snapped out, hitting my right shoulder hard enough that I staggered. I didn't fall, though. I *couldn't* fall. If I did, they'd catch me. Drag me back to the mafia boss.

I'd never be seen again.

Mom wouldn't miss me. My cousin wouldn't know or care. Only a few friends might ask where I was and why I up and left without selling my one-room apartment.

Breaking free of the Vessar, I wrenched forward. I ran faster, fleeing around the corner with enormous city buildings looming around me. Shuttles zipped overhead, low enough that the breeze from their passage made my long hair whip my face. I shoved it aside as I bolted onto the main thoroughfare, shoving people and various aliens aside.

My pace slowed when I reached the lifted sidewalk. I shot a glance over my shoulder. The Vessars followed, their three eyes keeping me in sight. They ignored the goods on display in shops lining the right side of the walk.

If I were lucky, I'd lose them in the open market ahead. They could be relentless, but I had patience and determination. I'd outlast them.

A Vessar came up close behind me, his low hissing voice raking down my spine. "Come wit usssss. We be kind."

Like I'd believe something like that? There was nothing kind about being sold.

"I'm a free citizen," I said, hoping the creature didn't hear the shake in my voice. "This is Jake's problem. You have no right to come after me."

"Gives creditssss for cousin, and we leavessss."

I could drain my account and sign over my next few year's earnings, but what would I use to live on after that? With only a rudimentary education, I couldn't secure a high-paying job. Ten years after moving out of Mom's house at eighteen, and I still wasn't much better off.

"Leave me alone," I said, keeping my voice soft. While some might rush to my defense if I screamed, others would crowd around and cheer while the Vessar mafia minions pinned me down and tied me up.

A suckered limb coiled around my arm. Bold of him, but no one was looking this way.

After prying the suction cups off my arm, I broke into a jog, darting around couples strolling and families pausing to gape through shop windows.

A sign ahead, Intergalactic Employment Agency, drew my eye. I wasn't looking for a job, but I could hide inside until the Vessars gave up and slunk away.

Maybe it was time I sold my apartment and moved to a distant colony. If I took care with my trail, the Vessars wouldn't be able to follow.

When I stepped inside the Agency, a monotone chime rang out overhead. A flat, disc-like hover computer zipped from the back room and hovered close to my face.

"Recognition proceeding," it said.

I struggled not to cringe. It would record that I'd been here and—

Tiny lights flashed behind its dark view screen. "Cora Marie Westmore has been entered into the database. I am now sorting for available positions that fit your experience."

"Thank you, um . . . I'm not sure I'm truly looking for a job, but I'm open to exploring possibilities." That sounded neutral enough.

I nudged the droid to the side and glanced through the clear plexi behind me. The Vessars were fuming on the walk, their dusky blue cheeks darkening. They flailed their limbs, smacking those who passed by. I doubted they'd dare enter the building, since they'd been forbidden to interfere in matters of general commerce.

They didn't leave as I'd hoped, however. One leaned against a metal post on the opposite side of the walk, and the other two smooshed their faces against the plexi, keeping me in sight.

Did this place have a back door I could escape through?

"Do you have live personnel working today?" I asked.

Anything to delay this process. If I remained here for hours, the Vessars might give up.

"I can page someone," the droid said. "However, I am well programmed and delighted to share job options with you. I note in your bio that you have considerable construction experience."

If you could count the carpenter's assistant job that I'd done for four years in my early twenties. The job was on Stellar 4, and despite the filter dome overhead, I'd gotten sunburned. As a bonus, I'd also gained ripped muscles, though I wasn't sure they'd hung around for long after I quit.

"Yes," I said when lights flashed behind the droid's view screen. It continued to hover in front of my face. "I do have construction experience. I've done all kinds of jobs, actually."

"Delightful. We have five positions open within this quadrant that suit your skills."

"What about," another look outside showed the damn Vessars still waiting. A growl ripped through me. How long would it take for them to give up?

"Two of these positions ask that the applicant arrive immediately," the droid continued. "A shuttle will transport you directly from here."

I frowned. "Like, *here*, here?"

"That is correct."

"What about my apartment?" I'd worked hard to buy it. I wouldn't abandon it to whoever chose to claim it.

"It would be secured until you returned."

"And my current job?"

"We have applicants waiting for this type of position."

It only paid a few credits more than minimum wage, but times were tough. No one was irreplaceable.

If I accepted a position off world, I'd escape the Vessars. I could arrange for my property to be sold and the credits deposited in my account. I wouldn't have to return to this city, and if I was lucky, the Vessars wouldn't discover where I'd gone.

The Vessars couldn't threaten a droid to give up this kind of information.

My mood perked up.

"Tell me more about the openings," I said.

"The first is in the Tricar Quadrant and involves—"

"Nope."

"Excuse me?" It whirled backward, huffing with pretend dismay.

Really, these droids were too lifelike. Creepy even. That's what the government wanted: friendly computers to make life pleasant for us citizens.

"The Tricar Quadrant is an icy wasteland," I said.

"The position pays well."

And we all knew why. "Tell me about the second position."

"A construction assistant position with a colony manager on planet Merth 4X7, helping build their residence."

A house on a distant colony, then. "I don't think I've heard of Merth . . ."

"4X7 is located in the Sebula Quadrant. A different

individual had been hired for this position, but they abruptly backed out before the task could be concluded." The droid grumbled, though they didn't have true feelings. They were just programmed to act like they did.

It launched into a spiel to sell the job. "Merth 4X7 is an agricultural planet with three colonies, primarily growing hemp. Indigenous populations, none. Settlers, three thousand twenty-two, though few reside in the colony with this position. Water, potable. Air, breathable. Gravity is approximate to this planet. As far as the employer, the last to hold this position reported he—"

"The job sounds perfect," I jumped in to say as Vessar claws scraped down the plexi behind me. Would they be that daring?

With only the droid present, they might. I doubted a machine working at an employment agency was programmed to provide defense. The government wouldn't expect them to need something like that.

Nope, the droid would either watch while the Vessars took me, and then say nothing, or protest only to be reprogrammed by the lizard mafia to forget what happened.

"I'll take the second position," I said. "Transport me now."

"Of course," the droid said. A thin panel projected from beneath its viewing screen. "Please sign here."

I scrawled my name.

A hum erupted in the back of the small room, and a transport pod thumped down against the floor, coming to a stop. The hatch peeled open across the front.

"You will be transported in suspension, as Merth 4X7 is twenty-seven-point-two light years from Earth," the droid said.

Lovely. I'd only traveled in suspension a few times, and I'd been dizzy when I woke up. Still, this job would get me off Earth and away from the Vessar lizard mafia, hopefully forever.

"What's my boss's name?" I asked.

The droid paused, then spit it out. "Kreelevar Nohmal Trirag Grikohr."

"Say that one fast."

"Excuse me?"

The Vessars jangled the front door handle.

"It doesn't matter." Panic lifted my voice. "Get me out of here. Now."

The door slammed opened, and the Vessars tumbled into the room, slipping on the tiles, and falling to the floor in a scramble of tangled, suction cup limbs.

"Of course," the droid said, glancing at the Vessars. "I will be with you shortly once I've made arrangements for this human." It turned back to me. "Thank you for stopping by. We at the Intergalactic Employment Agency appreciate your enthusiasm."

"Yeah, that's it. I'm wicked excited." I rushed to the pod and jumped inside. The hatch closed, and straps looped across my body, then tightened. A pinch on my arm was followed by my head spinning.

The Vessars clawed across the room, their limbs reaching toward me.

"Haha. You lose," I shouted, though I doubted they'd hear through the plexi shuttle lid.

My laugh echoed around me as the pod shot up through the chute, leaving the Vessars and my cousin's debt behind.

# 2

## KREEL

As I attached another solar roof shingle to my still-under-construction home, I grumbled. When I agreed to come to this planet to help build residences and centers of commerce, then provide oversight of the settlers, I was told I would be assigned an assistant.

Instead, I'd poured the foundation and erected the frame by myself. Now I was roofing the place without an assistant in sight. I wasn't opposed to hard labor; the fates knew I'd done plenty of it through my yarling years in the mine I'd discovered on my home planet. Extracting jewels from the soil had built muscle and filled my bank account with credits. But that was a job for yarlings, not a thirty-something orc like me.

When I contacted the employment agency immediately after I arrived on Merth 4X7, I was told they'd send someone right away. They had, but the foolish human quit. A recent missive told me a second assistant was on their way.

Sunlight poured down, overheating my skin. It didn't help that my roofing materials were designed to suck in the light. Once connected to my home, I'd appreciate the generated power, but right now, I'd turned into a conduit between the solar shingles and the sun.

A gust of wind would be welcome, but so far, it remained scarce, which could be due to the surrounding tall vegetation.

As if someone heard my thought, a stiff breeze swept across the valley, reaching me at the top of the hill overlooking the town. I paused and savored the thrill of the sweat drying on my thick skin. It wouldn't be long before I was soaked through again. I'd already shucked my shirt and wore only pants that hung low on my waist.

This colony spanned five thousand hickars, which meant it would take nearly a complete sun to cross to the other side on foot. I'd constructed the frame of my home far enough away from town to keep the noise from reaching me, yet close enough I could stop in and make sure all the villagers were behaving.

After laying a row of shingles, I leapt off the roof to the ground to collect a few more bundles.

I gnashed my tusks, frustrated that this day appeared to be ending without anyone arriving. It was making me cranky. Or *crankier* I supposed a few might say. I'd . . . developed a reputation in town already.

A barbarian brute, one or two had called me.

Asshole, the rest whispered behind my back.

Was it my fault I required order and obedience? If everyone did their jobs correctly the first time, they'd never hear a word from me. And if they listened to how I wanted everything organized, we could prevent problems rather than leaving me to clean up after something fell apart or a dam broke and flooded the entire valley. The latter hadn't happened. Yet.

Hefting two packs of shingles, I stepped onto the lift, and it projected me up, stopping when it was level with the roof trusses. I tossed the packets onto the sub-roof and jumped over them, my boots making dull thuds on the rough surface when I landed.

I worked through the afternoon, and my grumbles were beaten back by hard labor. When I finished for the day, I'd call the employment agency again. If they didn't send an assistant by midday tomorrow, I would contact someone else.

The fates must be irritated with me. Clouds formed overhead. A crack and a boom, and rain poured down, soaking my skin and making my pants stick to my frame.

As the rain continued, I laid roof shingles, snarling and snapping at each one, though they weren't to blame for my growly attitude.

The rain eventually ceased. Soon, I steamed in the blazing sunlight again, and I almost missed the cooling rain.

A hum erupted overhead, and I paused, watching as a pod appeared, flying toward my location.

Maybe the employment agency hadn't failed me after all.

When the shuttle landed on my scraggly front lawn, I

stood and leapt off the roof, landing easily on the ground.

I strode over to the pod just as it opened, and it was a good thing I did.

A human female tumbled out of the opening.

Before she could collapse on the ground, I scooped her up in my arms.

# 3
## CORA

A muscular, teal-green orc carried me across a scruffy lawn. His blocky face was highlighted with two-inch tusks jutting up past his thick, lighter green lips. A broad, hairless unibrow gave way to black, band-like ridges lining his forehead. Five-inch blunted horns jutted up from his head through long bands of whitish hair.

"Put me down," I squeaked, squirming. I was being kidnapped by a giant orc, and he was taking me to . . . I wasn't sure where he was taking me, but I didn't want to hang around and find out.

"You nearly collapsed," he growled, coming to a standstill, and scowling down at me.

"Cranky, aren't you?"

His scowl deepened. "I rescued you."

"I'm not a damsel in distress."

"I do not know that term." He did, however, lower

me to my feet. When they nearly gave way, he huffed and lifted me again, cradling me in his arms.

"You're an orc, aren't you?" I asked, pegging him by his appearance. A variety of orc species had formed colonies in this quadrant. I'd read about it on the news.

"I am a Thoksas warrior."

"And you're settling on this planet?"

"Why are you here?" he bellowed. His face darkened, and his ears wiggled. They might be rounded like mine on the bottom, but a small nub dangled from the tip, though it didn't sway with his movement.

"*Where* am I?" I peered around, taking in the partly finished building, a high fence, and thick woods beyond. We stood on a hill overlooking a cozy village nestled in the valley below. Buildings in yellow, pink, and baby blue dotted the area. Wait. This was a colony.

Ding, ding, ding. It was all coming back to me.

"Is this Merth 4X7?" I asked.

He jerked his head forward, but he said nothing.

"I took a new job as a construction assistant, and the shuttle was supposed to deliver me to my new boss."

"What is your boss's name?" he growled.

He truly was cranky. I had no idea why his butt was twisted into a wad, and I had no desire to find out.

"I took a job with Kreelevar Noo . . . scral? Tire, something."

He gnashed his tusks. "Kreelevar *Nohmal Trirag Grikohr.*"

I pointed my finger at him. "That's it."

He stared at my finger, and because I got the idea that he'd bite it off if I pissed him off, I yanked it back and tucked it beneath my ass.

"I am Kreelevar Nohmal Trirag Grikohr, but you are *not* my assistant."

When I wiggled, he put me down again, and I was grateful my brain had stopped spinning and my legs supported me.

I lifted my chin. "Well, you see, I *am* your new assistant. You paid my passage, and I'm here, ready to strap on a tool belt, heft a hammer, and help you build . . ." I waved to the building and plastered a cheery grin on my face. "I assume that's your new home?"

"I will send you back," he growled. "You are not the assistant I am looking for."

I lifted my arms and made muscles. "I'm stronger than I look." I needed to remain here until things cooled down with the lizard mafia back on Earth. "I've got carpentry experience too!"

"You are not the assistant I am seeking," he said again.

I pouted. "Won't you give me a chance? I promise I'll work hard. You won't regret hiring me."

His fists smacked onto his hips, and I slid my gaze down his teal-green, muscular front. Muscles and muscles and muscles, completely bare all the way to his low-slung pants—how had I missed his naked chest while he held me? His big muscles had given birth to teenage muscles, and they marched down his belly in segments.

If I dared, I'd trace my finger between them, though I had a feeling he'd swat my hand away.

His waist cut in tight, and I struggled not to drool. It would be a big mistake to fall in lust or anything else with my new boss. We needed to keep this relationship professional.

"You will climb back into the pod and return to wherever you came from," he roared.

I should be afraid of him. After all, he was twice my size, he had ten times—at least—my muscle mass, and he was super snarly. I did have construction experience, but it wasn't recent. It was a guarantee I'd make a mistake, and he'd bite my head off. Literally. His tusks looked sharp enough to do it.

"You can huff all you like, but I'm not going anywhere." I put my hands on my hips, mimicking his gesture, though it lost its effect because I was tiny compared to him.

"You will." He pivoted, but only took one step away before coming to a quick stop.

Following, I nearly ran into his back—that I noted was equally muscly.

I stepped away as he spun back to face me.

"What did you do with it?" His voice grew in volume. "What did you do with the shuttle?"

"Um . . ." I lifted my eyebrows and pointed at the pod zipping toward the planet's outer atmosphere. "I think you're stuck with me, Kreelevar."

"Kreel!"

"Kreel it is, then. It appears I'm here to stay." I held

out my hand. "Shall we shake on our new business arrangement?"

# 4
## KREEL

The Intergalactic Employment Agency had made a mistake. When I'd filled out the application, I'd insisted they send a male, not a puny human female.

A female who could make my body . . .

I snarled, not wanting to think about it. She wasn't Thoksas, which meant she couldn't possibly trigger my frenzy.

Realizing this fact cooled my irritation. I removed my fists from my hips and dropped them to my sides.

With the transport pod gone, there wasn't anything I could do to remove her from my presence, at least for today. She indicated she had construction experience. I desperately needed an assistant. I could give her a rising sun or two to see if this would work out.

If it didn't, I'd book her a one-way return flight back to wherever she came from.

"I feel like we got off on the wrong foot," she said.

I stared at her miniscule feet, wondering how things

so stubby could support her weight. She *had* staggered when she first arrived. Perhaps her feet were defective.

Just my luck to hire a defective assistant.

Her hand jutted toward me. "I'm Cora. Cora Westmore. It's nice to meet you."

I stared at her hand. What did one do with a limb that was projected?

"Okay, um, sure," she said, her hand dropping to her thigh. "Anyway, I'm here to help, and that's what I'm going to do."

I sighed, feeling as if I had little say in this. How had this female taken over the situation so quickly? From the time my parents died when I was three and our clan leader took me into his dwelling, I'd learned to handle any situation. When someone wanted to cut off my arm, I ducked. Another tried to burn me alive, and I jumped into the river.

It was only when I turned twelve and one of the other orphans tried to behead me that I learned the best way to handle this sort of situation was to fight back. Life had gotten easier after that.

If someone attacked, I'd easily deflect them. If they lifted a weapon, I could deploy tactics that would disarm them within a tick.

I wasn't sure how to handle this female.

"We will see how this goes," was all I was willing to say.

"You're going to love having me help," she gushed. Turning, she stared toward my future dwelling. "Gorgeous. You've done this all by yourself?"

My chest puffed with pride. I'd worked hard, and my home did look attractive. "I had help at first, but they quit." Within an hour, actually, but she didn't need to know that.

"I see you're installing solar roof panels." She tapped her temple. "Wise."

Heat filled my face, an odd feeling. "It is practical."

"Still, I bet you've incorporated other energy efficient components into your home."

"I have." Now I was nearing the point of gushing. Why? It made no sense. I was a simple male. Some had called me surly, though I wasn't sure why. My moods remained stable. It wasn't my fault everyone around me didn't take life seriously.

"Are you living on-site?" she asked.

"I am." This would be a problem. Another male could take a side of my tent, and we'd make do.

Growing up with many orphans within the leader's dwelling, it was common for males to room together. When I discovered the mine, I'd lived there by myself. If I'd told anyone about it, they would've gutted me and stolen my jewels.

"Perfect. Sleeping on-site means we can get started bright and early in the morning." She flashed me a smile.

"Are you always this cheery?"

"Are you always this grumpy?" Humor bubbled in her voice, though, again, I wasn't sure why.

"This is me." I spread my hands wide.

"It's okay," she said. "You're growing on me."

I didn't understand half of what this female said, but

if she could nail roof tiles down, I'd keep her around a bit before making my final decision.

"All righty, then," she said, rocking back on her heels.

I grabbed her arm to keep her from toppling over.

She frowned down at my hand, and I snapped it back to my side.

"Nice claws," she said. "Bet you could open a can of beans with that thumb."

I lifted my hand, studying my thumb claw. "Doesn't everyone have them?"

"Nope." She displayed fingers with claws as blunted as her useless teeth.

"Did you have them filed?" I asked, truly curious. How did a being like this survive? Was it some kind of bizarre human fashion statement?

"Only when they start growing long."

"I see." I didn't, but it truly didn't matter. We'd find a way to make this work. I was determined to get my roof finished with the next few risings of the sun.

Sighing, I peered around. I'd show her to our shared quarters, and she could put away her things.

"Where are your possessions?" I asked. The pod should've ejected them before departing.

"That's the thing," she said, glancing toward the sky. "I left Earth in a hurry, and all I've got are the clothes on my back. I don't suppose I could borrow a comb and a toothbrush?" She bared her blunted teeth again, something that puzzled me. If she had majestic tusks like me, and she flashed them like that, I'd take it as a challenge.

I doubted this small being would dare do such a thing to a hardened orc like me.

"What is a . . . toothbrush?" I asked.

She ran the tip of her finger across her tiny teeth, wiggling her finger back and forth. "Thoothbroosh." One of her eyebrows lifted, an interesting trick. My brow lifted as one unit, and mine did not sprout bushy . . . hair. That was the term. I'd heard of eyebrows before, though I'd never seen them in real life.

Her finger dropped from her mouth. "Never mind. I'll figure it out. As for clothing, I'm sure you've got some old stuff around I can wear, right?"

I was more than twice her size. My shirt would float across her curvy body, and my pants would need considerable rope to keep the waistband at her hips.

Wait . . . Curvy body? Why was I noticing such a thing? I didn't find her attractive.

Did I?

Fuck, maybe I did.

No matter. I wouldn't act on it. Our incompatibility was one reason. If I tried to mate with her, I'd crush her.

"I will obtain you clothing," I finally said. "If you remain in my employ."

"Aw, don't be like that," she said, pursing her pale pink lips—another oddity I'd never seen before. Other than the villagers who were not human, everyone I knew had green skin, green lips, and pale white bands on their heads.

"Don't be like what?" She sauntered right up to me, stopping before our bodies touched—thank the fates. I wasn't sure how I'd handle that. "This is going to be fun. I promise. I'll help you build your house, and then I'll find another job and get out of your hair."

"I do not have . . . hair."

Frowning at my likarns, she tapped her chin. "You're right. It's a figure of speech. It means I'll leave here, and you won't have to think about me again."

For some reason, I worried I would be thinking of this female long after she was gone.

# 5
## CORA

Kreel was kinda cute in an orc-like way. Actually, he was a Thoksas. I needed to remember that. The last thing I wanted to do was say something disrespectful to my new boss.

Still . . . He was cute from his teal-green skin to his tail, his thumb claws, and his blunted horns that I strangely wanted to touch. Stroke even.

And where had that thought come from? We were completely different species. He was twice my size. If we tried to fuck, he'd split me in two.

Well, unless he had a puny cock. I was not going to ask. I might meander across others' boundaries, but I wasn't *completely* uncivilized.

"I will show you where you will sleep tonight," he finally said.

I got the idea that he had no clue what to do with me. He'd soon see I was a hard worker. I'd show him how important it was to keep me on the job until it was finished. By then, the Vessars would've lost my trail.

I followed him around the right side of the building and up to the small rustic tent. Could a person stand upright, or would they hit their head on the top? It was going to be cozy if we both tried to squeeze inside.

"Cute," I said when he stopped in front of it and released the door fastenings.

"Cute?"

His ass, but I wouldn't mention that. "I meant the tent." His must be around here somewhere. I assumed this was the one his prior assistant used.

He caught my gaze trained on his bod and scowled.

I pressed a neutral smile on my face. "Are you going to show me inside?"

"Ah, yes," he said, turning back to the tent. Stooping, he shouldered his way through the opening, and I followed.

There was only one big bed in the center with only the width of a foot or so around it.

"I'll sleep here?" I asked. It wasn't much, but I could call it home until I left. Once I'd cleaned the place up and aired the bedding, I could store my clothing in the tiny space between the bed and the outer walls. When I had clothes, that was.

He scowled. "This is my tent."

"Okay, so where will *I* sleep?" I cringed at the floor that looked like an army wearing muddy boots had stomped across it.

"I will . . . I will . . ." His face darkened. "We will not sleep together."

"I'm glad you've pointed that out." He wasn't *that* cute.

"I will sleep . . . outside," he said. "For tonight. Tomorrow, I will go into town and bring back a second tent."

"All right." If this were a romance novel, something I'd read plenty of back on Earth, I'd tell him we could share the bed. It was big. Neither of us would know the other person was there.

This wasn't a romance novel. Although, Kreel would make a nice hero. Me as the heroine? I was too snarky. Readers enjoyed sympathetic women, not ones like me.

"Thank you," I added when he did nothing but stare at me.

"We will get you clothing tomorrow as well."

"That's very generous of you."

"I will, of course, take the cost from your wages," he said. While his tone remained solemn, his dark green eyes sparkled. I couldn't tell if he was joking. Why would he? He'd been a snarly orc from the moment I met him.

"I expect you to," I said. A nice, neutral reply.

"For now, we must work. The rainy season comes soon, and I must have my roof in place."

"Then let's get to it," I said with enthusiasm. I'd actually enjoyed my construction job. It might be fun to help Kreel finish his home.

I followed him to the lift and up onto the roof.

"Do you have an extra hammer?" I asked, looking around.

He handed me something the size of a sledgehammer.

I tried to hold on to it, but it dragged my arm down, making the hammer end thud on the sub-roof.

"You've got a big hammer," I said. "I can see why you want me to hold it."

His face darkened, though I had no idea why.

"Yes," he said. "I have a big hammer."

Oh. Attack of the sexy thoughts. My face got hot.

I needed to fight my awareness of this guy. He was dangerous. If I wasn't careful...

Nope, nope, nope. I wasn't going to let my brain go in that direction.

"Do you have a smaller hammer?" I asked, struggling to keep my tone professional. Truly, I wanted to say something dirty.

Maybe I already had.

"I do." He jumped down to the ground and returned via the lift with a hammer about half the size of the first. "This should fit you well."

Dirty, dirty thoughts swirled through my mind. "I'm sure it will . . . fit me fine."

He gulped, and his gaze shot down my frame. What did he think of me? I didn't dare ask.

Business first.

"Since we're laying solar shingles," I said. "Do you want me to start banging on the other end and meet up with you in the middle?"

"Banging . . ." His eyes smoldered, telling me where his mind was going.

My body burst into flames. He hadn't touched me in that way, and he never would. If nothing else, I could sense he wouldn't take advantage of me.

"Yes, I'll, um, go do some banging," I said, needing to get away from his heated gaze ASAP.

"Yes, do that," he said dryly.

I hefted a clump of shingles from the pile on the roof and scurried as far away from him as I could get before lowering my materials on the sub-roof.

"Do a good job," he called out.

I couldn't resist one parting shot. "No worries. I know exactly how to bang by myself."

# 6

## KREEL

My skin trembled, and my hearts thudded in unison, ramming themselves against my ribcage. My cock bucked beneath my trousers like a beast desperate to get free.

There wasn't a damn thing I was going to do about my arousal.

Cora wasn't interested in me, and I'd found nothing attractive in her.

Still, I couldn't keep from watching her out of the corner of my eye. I laid shingles, but I was hyperaware of her working on the opposite side of the roof.

Since I was her boss, I needed to supervise her, correct?

I rose and strode over to where she worked, hovering over her, actually. She kept laying shingles, and being a perfectionist, I was satisfied with how she placed them and hammered them into the right position.

Her ass jutted toward me as she stooped forward,

tapping the hammer against the links connecting each segment together.

She had a nice ass for a puny human. Rounded and lush. I supposed her species might prefer her skinnier, though I hadn't met a human before her. I had seen vids, however, of slender females slinking across open areas with long dresses swirling around their ankles. Formal functions, but that was it.

A mine worker didn't take part in social niceties, not when, at any given time, someone might kill me.

She hummed as she worked, and I wasn't sure what to make of it.

"You are making sounds. You should stop," I said.

"You've got a delightful pair of coconuts," she bellowed out in song. "They sway and swing when you walk!"

I grumbled. She continued to sing about how too many bottles of rum made her dizzy. Her voice wasn't unpleasant, but the song was disruptive.

"Stop," I said.

Her voice got louder.

"Stop!"

Her voice cut off. Turning, she flopped onto her luscious ass. She swiped the golden bands off her face. Pulling something from her pocket, she secured the bands at the top of her head, leaving a long swath swinging across her back.

I stood there, gaping at her, analyzing her every move. Why did she fascinate me this much?

"What if I like to sing while I work?" she finally asked. "It makes the time go by quickly."

"You must not do so." I said it in all seriousness.

"Why?"

"Because it is disruptive."

"Who am I disrupting?" she asked, with a scrunch of her forehead.

"Me. It is distracting."

"Ah." Her head tilted, and she shaded her eyes as she looked up at me. "I distract you?"

"Yes. No."

"Now that's decisive."

I growled. "Do not sing."

"Is that a condition of my employment?"

Frowning, I thought about it for a long while. Could I make such a demand?

"I'd say you can't decide, so I win." Her face cleared, and she rose to her feet. She tipped her head back and burst into song, a tune about little males dancing through a stream. They had big zucchinis, though I had no idea what a zucchini could be.

She pivoted and started working on the roof again, swaying her delectable ass to her tune.

I grumbled and returned to work, where I struggled to ignore her, but couldn't. Her song sunk into my mind and when she finished, I found myself repeating it over and over.

"I thought we're not allowed to sing," she said with a laugh from beside me.

"I am not singing," I said, laying another shingle and

securing it to the others. Rocking back on my heels, I scanned the roof. "If we push hard, we will meet in the middle before sunset."

"When do we eat?"

"Not now."

"I'm hungry. I left in a hurry. Avoiding being sold, and all that. I didn't have anything to eat before that."

"Being sold?" I asked, focusing on that part of her statement.

"We'll forget I said that."

I couldn't, though I wouldn't speak of it again. "Why not?"

"Why not what?" she asked.

"Why did you not eat before you left?" I shouted.

"I was in a hurry. A few guys were . . . nothing."

I slanted a glance at the sky. "I suppose we could stop early."

Her eyes lit up. "Awesome. What's for dinner?"

"You expect me to feed you in addition to clothing and housing you?"

Her face fell, and my belly churned with regret. "You're right. You don't owe me a thing I can . . . forage later." She pivoted and returned to the diminished pile of shingles, lifting one.

With a heavy sigh, I stood. "I will prepare food."

"I can find it for myself, thank you very much," she snipped.

Did this refer back to her taking care of all her needs herself? I should not be thinking of her lying on my bed, her body writhing with pleasure.

My cock jerked upward, eager to participate if sex was on the menu.

"Why do you keep getting a stiffy?" she asked, her gaze zoned in on my crotch.

"I do not have a . . . stiffy."

She huffed. "Erection. Hard-on. Woody. Boner. Love muscle. Anaconda."

"I prefer that term."

Her head tilted. "What?"

"You can call mine an anaconda."

Her gaze shot to my groin. "Jeez, dude. You ever heard of sexual harassment?"

# 7
## CORA

I was just teasing, but still. This guy . . . He kept my head spinning, and I had a feeling I wouldn't return to the ground for a very long time. Figuratively speaking, since we were still on the roof.

"It must be . . . hard to walk around with an anaconda inside your pants. Does it bang on your belly?"

Bang . . . I really needed to stop using words that added fuel to the fire Kreel had lit.

He grunted and gave me a heavy stare that must be common with orcs. Like everything else about him, it was cute. "My anaconda prefers to *bang* elsewhere."

Touché.

"I will return." His hard-on persisted, but he turned away and headed for the lift. Instead of using it to reach the ground, he jumped, landing with a solid thump. He hefted an ax and strode to the right of the building, continuing into the woods.

I wasn't sure I wanted to know what he planned to do with that ax.

After laying another row of shingles, I realized I had to pee. Kreel hadn't returned from his adventure in the woods, but that gave me time to take care of business.

I took the ladder down and walked around, looking for anything that might serve as a porta potty. Unfortunately, I didn't find anything.

With a sigh, I strode closer to the woods on the left side of the house and peered into the dark vegetation. Nothing moved. Kreel appeared to have run away to become a lumberjack. That should give me plenty of time.

I faced the house and tugged down my pants. Squatting, I let loose. Ugh, I really hated going au naturel, but what choice did I have?

After finding a leaf, I wiped. I straightened, tossing the leaf aside. A sound behind me sent me spinning.

Kreel strode along a path, exiting where I was standing, the ax in one hand and a fuzzy creature the size of a pony draped across his shoulders. Blood coiled down his chest from the slice in the creature's neck.

Seeing me standing with my pants around my ankles, he stopped. His mouth dropped open, and the ax fell from his hand, clunking on the forest floor.

I scrambled to yank up my pants, but it was too late.

Kreel gaped at my crotch. "You ... You ..."

I held up my hand. "Don't even go there. I had to pee. It's a fact of nature."

"Why not use the excrement facility? We are not

beasts."

That was debatable.

I appreciated the name, excrement facility. It worked better than bathroom since most used the bathroom for things other than bathing. "I don't know where it is." I fastened my pants and backed away from where I'd watered the plants.

He grunted and stooped down to lift his ax. Straightening, he strode past me, aiming for the building.

I followed, skipping to catch up and trot beside him. It took two of my steps for one of his. "What did you catch?" I wasn't squeamish; we all needed to eat.

"I killed a sublox."

"Ah, yes, of course."

He passed the tent and stopped at a big wooden table, tossing the dead sublox onto the surface.

I watched while he sliced into it, cleaning out parts from the belly I didn't want to closely examine. Where I came from, we ate meat, but we bought it in polite packages at the market.

"What kind of creature is a sublox?" I asked.

"The edible kind."

"That's good."

He sliced off chunks of meat and dropped them into a big, clean metal bowl he pulled out from beneath the table. After covering it with a cloth, he gathered the fur and innards and strode into the woods with them, returning a short time later to wash his hands in a bucket of water.

"Don't you worry about drawing predators to the

carcass?" I asked.

"That is the point."

"What point?"

"Those drawn in become tomorrow's meal."

Delightful. And I was sleeping inside a flimsy tent tonight, all alone. Maybe a single bed romance wasn't such a bad idea after all. Kreel was huge. Nothing would dare come near while he was around.

Pivoting away from me, he gathered kindling and lit a fire in a pit the size of a small shuttle.

"Rustic," I said, taking in the bloody table. Was there disinfectant around? I needed to locate it before I set out silverware and napkins.

"There is an excrement room inside my dwelling," he said. "But I have not installed the cooking quarters. That will come after the roof is completed. It'll be easier to work inside during the rainy season."

"How long do you anticipate it'll take to finish the house?" I tried not to gape as he lifted a log twelve inches across and eight feet long and threw it onto the fire.

"The span of fifty rising suns or so."

So, fifty days. That should be long enough for the Vessars to lose my scent. That thought perked me up nicely.

He lifted a metal grate and dropped it over the fire with a clatter. Sparks flew into the air, and the metal grate started to sizzle.

"What can I do to help?" I asked. "Can I make a salad or something to go with the sublox?"

"Why would I eat salad?" he asked, cocking his head

my way. He took the bowl of meat over and set it on a second, though smaller, table near the fire.

"Vegetables. Fiber. You know, all those important vitamins and minerals."

He grunted. "We eat meat."

"Only meat?"

"What else is there?"

"Cookies?" I asked.

"This is a veg-ee-table?"

"No, it's a sweet."

He gestured to his mouth. "Sweets will rot my majestic tusks."

"We can't have that, then." I sighed. No sweets? I was going to go out of my mind without my favorite indulgence. "Are we going to eat meat for every meal?"

"Of course. It makes an orc body strong."

If one was an orc. I was not. "It's boring. I'm an omnivore. Plus a cookie-a-vore when I'm PMSing." Which I wouldn't do for months, thanks to my implant.

"I eat meat." Lifting a thick slab of sublox, he dropped it onto the grate. Flames licked across it, and it started cooking immediately. The lovely essence of roasted meat filled the air.

In no time, he had twelve thick hunks sizzling over the fire. With a huge, long-handled fork, he flipped them. He pulled a pouch from his pocket and untied the top, then sprinkled a powder across the meat.

"Spices?" I asked.

"Salt."

Hefting the bucket of water, he dumped it across the

table and swished the water around with a cloth, washing off the bits of sublox.

He pulled two metal plates almost two feet across from a box underneath the table and laid them on the still-wet surface with a clatter. Hefting another, he returned to the fire and poked the fork into each, lifting them away from the flames and placing them on the platter.

He dropped it on the table and settled two chairs on either side, waving to one. "Sit. Eat. Don't complain."

"What would I complain about?" I asked, gingerly perching on the edge of the chair. It was so big; it could swallow me whole.

With a knife, he lifted a slab of meat bigger than my head and plopped it on my two-foot long metal plate.

"Enjoy," he said with a tusky smile I found strangely appealing.

I preferred eating meat that didn't look ready to leap off the plate and run back into the woods. And . . . it was silly, but I tried to stay civilized. I'd eaten with my hands. I'd dug through back-alley dumpsters behind restaurants, my belly a hollow cavern, trying to ignore the yummy smells drifting through the air. Trying to ignore the clink of silverware as those more fortunate than me dug into their meals.

I blinked at the cut of meat that was so raw, pink liquid oozed from where he'd stabbed the knife. Fending for myself for most of my life meant I would eat almost anything—and had more times than I liked. I should be thrilled to sink my teeth into this big cut of meat.

"Do you have a fork?" I asked.

Thick lines formed on Kreel's forehead. "What is a fork?"

"An eating utensil."

"We don't need anything like that." He lifted the slab he'd selected for himself to his mouth and ripped into it with his tusks.

How could I find this attractive? When he flashed a smile my way and chewed, nudging his head toward my meat, my body flooded with desire. It didn't make sense, but there it was. He was big, teal-ish green, and I found him hotter than all get out.

As for the meat?

I picked it up and bit into it, finding the cut tender, tasty, and with just the right amount of salt.

We finished. That is, he ate three hunks of meat while I chowed through as much of my first slice as I could.

Sitting back in his chair, he grinned again. "You are turning into an adequate assistant."

"Adequate?" I sputtered. "I'm an excellent assistant."

"That remains to be seen." He tugged a container out from under the table and placed the rest of the meat inside.

"Leftovers for breakfast?" I asked. When we went into town, I'd look for fruit and veggies. He might be able to survive on only meat, but my diet needed variety.

"I will place them in my cold storage."

"You've got a freezer?"

He frowned. "Cold storage."

"Okay," I said in a sunny voice. Really, did it matter what we called it?

He rose and carried the container into the house.

I followed. "Where's the, um, excrement room?"

As we traveled down a hall with unfinished walls made of timbers he'd cut in the woods, he tilted his head to an opening on the right.

No door, but I spied an enormous toilet-ish thing in the corner that would work for my needs.

He continued down the hall while I scooted inside and took care of business.

He was waiting in the front room when I came out, taking in the view from what I assumed would become a living room. Rolling hills stretched for as far as I could see, some peppered with tall trees, others pure open fields. The village nestled below.

"It's lovely here," I said. "I can see why you decided to join this colony."

"I took a job," he said. "Though I'm grateful my position gave me this." His hand swept out, encompassing the view and the structure he was building.

"How long will you remain here?"

"That remains to be seen. First, I must prove myself." His penetrating gaze met mine, and I sensed he was interested in what I might say to his words. "Do you understand this?"

"I believe so. I've spent much of my life trying to show everyone around me I'm a decent person, someone they'd like to know." I had friends. I wasn't completely alone. "My mom shoved me aside years ago, preferring to spend time with her friends and the boyfriend du jour. As for my nonexistent dad, he never gave me a chance."

"What do you mean?"

I shrugged. "He ditched Mom before I was born."

"Ah."

I couldn't read anything on Kreel's face. Why was I bringing this up? I should keep it hidden.

No. That wasn't true. My past was a part of me. I'd overcome it, refusing to let it beat me. I was no longer ashamed by how my parents had treated me. "I spent the years since I moved out of the home that I grew up in realizing I don't owe anyone anything. My feelings about myself were all that matter."

"That is admirable," he said softly. "We *are* alike."

"It's your insides that matter, not this." I pinched the skin on my arm. "This is just the package I'm wrapped up in. It's not who I truly am." I fisted my chest. "That's inside here."

"You are right."

His stern face didn't give anything away. For a second, I was worried I'd revealed too much and that I'd made myself vulnerable by doing so.

His gaze shot from mine to the ground. "I've been alone most of my life, despite being near others. For many years, I mined beneath the ground."

"You're about my age, right?"

He nodded.

I had a feeling a bombshell was about to explode between us. "When did you start mining?"

"When I was twelve."

# 8

## CORA

My eyes widened. I didn't know why I was stunned by his words. On Earth, the wealthy had passed laws long ago, lowering the age where a child was allowed to work. I'd gotten my first job at thirteen. "You started working in a mine when you were twelve?"

"It was that or remain at the leader's home, waiting for someone to kill me."

"Why would anyone want to kill a twelve-year-old? That's a little kid."

"Orphans compete with each other. I fought just like they did for meat, a place to sleep, even clothing."

I sagged against one of the interior studs. "Your parents didn't help you?"

"They died when I was three. The clan leader took me in, along with other orphans." Shadows lurked in his eyes, but he kept his jaw square. He gave me a curt nod. "I was not a . . . kid."

"Child."

"I knew what you meant."

I watched *him* now, more than the view. My tight chest made it difficult to breathe. "You grew up with orphans dying around you from fighting for things that should be given to them?"

"That is our way."

I'd struggled myself, but at least I'd had a place with my mom to lay my head at night. Food. Clothes. She hadn't doled out affection, but she didn't neglect my basic needs.

I couldn't imagine having to fight against other kids to survive. "It sounds like you had a rough life, and then it got worse. And then someone forced you to work in a mine."

He flashed a grim smile. "I found the mine. It was *mine*. The jewels I extracted allowed me to buy my own tent. Clothing. Food. I no longer had to fight for my right to exist. I moved out of the leader's house."

"If you had that, why come here?"

"All orc males must prove themselves."

"Mining didn't do that?"

"I didn't tell them," he said softly. "It was my mine, no one else's. If I shared, they would've killed me and stolen the jewels. When the lines tapped out, I applied for this position and came here. Once I prove myself to my people, I will be considered a true male. I can then relax and enjoy the life I'm creating here."

I thought I'd had it bad, but it was nothing like this. At least I'd had a decent home with Mom until I moved out as an adult.

"What you've done is admirable," I said through a tight throat.

He stiffened. "I've done what many others have before me. This is not anything to admire." Striding over to where a big window opening had been framed in the wall, he stared toward the valley. "This place will give me what I have craved all my life."

"Acceptance?"

"What else is there?"

Love. A family. I didn't have that myself, but it was something I hoped would happen.

I watched him while he looked out at the world he'd built with his own hands.

He might think he'd done nothing unusual, but I respected him now, when earlier, I'd thought he was just a pain in the ass.

Well, he still was a pain in the ass, but I had sympathy for him. Understanding. It softened my irritation with him.

Did he use a gruff demeanor to hide the pain from his rough upbringing?

Knowing about his past made me like him, something I hadn't expected to feel for a grumpy alien orc.

Finding him hot was one thing. I could ogle him when he wasn't looking and swipe away my drool. No touching, but his snarly manner made it easy to keep my hands to myself.

Picturing a small boy fighting with bigger kids, maybe crying because he was hungry, made him a more rounded person.

One I could care for.

I shook off the feeling. There would be no caring on this job. I was here to help him finish building his house. As soon as we finished, I'd leave.

He crossed the room, aiming for the open doorway leading outside. "It is getting dark."

While we'd talked, the sun had sunk closer to the horizon, shooting golden, streaky beams into the sky.

"We must prepare for bed," he added.

My little heart should not be tripping over itself because he'd mentioned the bed. He spoke in a general manner. We wouldn't be climbing beneath the covers together.

Why couldn't I stop remembering his thick cock kicking against the front of his pants?

Getting all horny for my boss could be dangerous.

I followed him across the big scruffy lawn. "Will you eventually clip this?" I asked as I scampered up to half-run beside him. I wasn't sure where he was going, but I was willing to go along for the ride—so to speak.

"Why would I cut it?"

"Because that'll make it look tidy."

"It is tidy just as it is. Nature makes it the way it is supposed to be."

I'd never thought of it that way. "I guess you're right."

"I'm always right." He crested a hill and stopped. Below, a wide river snaked out of the woods and toward the valley. It flowed along the side of the colorful town.

"Will you plant flowers?" I asked. "Landscape the area?"

He sighed. "You ask many questions."

"I'm curious. And flowers are pretty."

He blinked slowly. "I do not find them pretty. They are useless. I might, perhaps, plant things I can eat."

"So you do eat veggies."

"On occasion." His tusks flashed, though briefly. It was enough to knock the air right out of my lungs.

I poked his side, finding only muscle. "You're not a pure carnivore after all." I hadn't seen many guys with muscles in this location. Abs, yeah. Their backs if they worked out a lot. Arms and thighs, certainly.

Obliques, I think these rippling babies were called.

"I have even been known to eat a random piece of fruit," he said, starting down the hill.

"But no sweets."

"They rot the tusks."

I bared my teeth. "I eat my weight in sweets all the time, and I still have my choppers."

He touched one of my teeth. "Useless things, aren't they?"

"They chewed through that slab of meat."

"You ate almost nothing." His creased face suggested he was concerned about the idea, but this was cranky Kreel. He didn't care about me.

I shouldn't feel mushy because this burly orc was concerned. "I'm full. I couldn't eat another bite."

"You must eat more. Grow bigger and stronger."

My snort slipped out. "I'm fully grown, twenty-eight-years-old. I'm big enough, thank you very much. If anything, I could stand to lose a few pounds." Or twenty. Thirty. I wasn't going there with Kreel.

"No," he huffed. "You are not lush enough."

Lush? Had he actually been looking? Oh, my. I fanned my face, not sure what I thought about that. He was my boss, I repeated in my mind. He was an orc, though that didn't matter to me. He was enormous. We weren't physically or emotionally compatible.

As I followed him closer to the river, checking out his muscular butt outlined by his pants, I had to admit something to myself.

I was beginning to like Kreel.

# 9
## KREEL

I stopped beside the river, and the tiny, not-lush-enough human female paused with me.

"It's pretty here," she said, looking around.

"Pretty this, lovely that. Aesthetics are useless in life."

She gasped, but her twinkling eyes suggested she wasn't offended. "No, they're not."

"Tell me how they can be useful."

"Well, if you . . ."

"See?" I said with a pleased huff. "You cannot think of anything."

"Give me a second, would ya?" Her face cleared. "What if you wanted to go on a date?"

"A date of what?"

"Like take someone somewhere for romance."

I scowled. "Why would I wish to do something like that?"

"Don't you want to share your life with someone?

Maybe have children? Grow old with someone by your side?"

"I have never contemplated something like that. I assume if I meet my fated one, we'll realize it, and we will . . . fuck? I am not sure what else."

Her laugh snorted out hard enough that she bent over while her belly shook. "Funny." Straightening, she wiped her eyes.

They sparkled, and I had to admit they were pretty. Not that I'd ever speak that thought aloud. This pesky female could turn me into mush if I let her.

I bent forward and untied my boots.

"My point is, if you want to be with someone, you might want to give them flowers while you were . . . wooing them. I'm not sure that's a term you're familiar with."

I grumbled. "I am not a complete beast. Of course, I understand the term *wooing*." With a huff, I kicked away my boots and peeled off my socks, laying them across the side of my footwear.

She frowned at my toes. "Do your toe claws ever slice through your socks?"

"I file them, so they don't."

"Why leave them this long, then?"

I looked down at my wiggling toes, taking in my claws jutting out nicely from the ends of my toes. "In my species' past, toe claws could make the difference in battle."

"Did you use them in your mine?"

"Sometimes."

"But now you file them."

"I don't believe I'll need my toe claws to defend myself here."

"There are no dangerous predators in the area?" she asked, hooking her arms around her waist and shivering.

I lifted my hands, displaying the claws on each thumb. "That's what these are for. I wear boots on my feet."

"Except now."

"My toes enjoy breathing."

She chuckled. "They don't have lungs."

"Don't your toes enjoy being out in the air?"

"I suppose." She frowned at her footwear.

I undid the top of my pants.

"My point is." She didn't look up. "If you want to woo someone, you might want to give him or her flowers."

I pondered this thought while I continued to unfasten my pants. "I hadn't thought of that. Perhaps I should grow flowers, as ugly as they are." Then, if I met my fated one, I could give them something . . . pretty. Such a strange notion.

"See? I proved there's a use for things that look nice. Paintings also look nice, and they can lead to conversation. If there's a painting from a place you or the person you're wooing have visited, seeing that scene can make you smile. They say smiles add to your lifespan."

"Who says this?"

She shrugged. "Everyone."

"I do not."

Her eyebrows lifted. "Then you should."

I grumbled. "This is a concept I have never considered."

"Look at your roof shingles," she said, waving her hand in that direction. "They're uniformly laid out in a pattern that will look attractive when we're finished."

"This is how they need to be installed."

"But they'll look good," she insisted.

My brain scrambled through thoughts I'd never considered. I wasn't sure I liked it. "You shouldn't make me think."

She laughed again; her face wreathed with a smile that . . .

Fuck. It made her attractive.

Enough of that.

I tugged down my pants, pooling them around my ankles, then stepped out of them. Like always, I wore nothing beneath.

"What the hell are you doing?" she asked, her fingers fluttering on her lips, her wide-eyed gazed focused on my cock.

Odd how her simple glance could stir me. I'd had more hard-ons today than in more than a lunar cycle.

My cock jerked upright, eager to be planted inside . . . Cora.

Double fuck.

"I am bathing," I said, striding down the bank. The sooner I entered the cool water, the better. "You are welcome to join me or remain foul-smelling."

# 10

## CORA

My heart flailed behind my ribcage, and heat swirled through my body, pooling between my legs.

No. I wasn't getting hot for him. He was from a different species. He had claws on his toes and thumbs, and he was at least twice my size.

His cock was enormous. I'd looked. It rippled with veins, and I doubted he'd be able to get even the thick head inside me.

My body said it wouldn't mind giving it a try.

Bad body.

He wasn't offering. He despised me. It was clear he didn't find me attractive.

I watched as he waded into the water until it reached his chest. He kicked off and dove beneath the surface, not rising until he'd reached the middle. His head bobbed up, and he looked in this direction.

I felt the weight of his gaze. Did he expect me to strip off my clothing and join him?

Foul-smelling, he'd said, and he was right. I'd worked in the sun all afternoon, and my pits wouldn't pass a sniff test inspection. But take off all my clothing?

I could avoid him when I was in the water. It was a big river.

He wouldn't truly watch me remove my clothing.

Without peering his way, and without turning around—something I nearly cringed and did—I tugged my shirt over my head. I wore a bra beneath. It matched my pink panties. They were silly things with little flowers adorning the silky fabric. I might wear utilitarian clothing on the outside, but I liked feeling pretty beneath.

They were wasted on Kreel.

That thought gave me courage. I slipped out of my sneakers and socks, then tugged down my pants. When I looked up, I found him washing his face and head. He wasn't looking; I was the one only thinking about sex.

I really needed to stop thinking about Kreel and sex in the same sentence. But that cock . . .

I unfastened my bra and dropped it onto my pants, then shimmied out of my panties.

When I strode down the bank to enter the water, I found Kreel had swam closer.

He stared at me, his jaw unhinged and his big green eyes wide.

Before my eyes, medium gray tribal markings that

looked like swirling tattoos appeared on his upper arms and shoulders, as if an invisible artist etched them into his skin

This wasn't possible.

Seeing them stunned me enough that I stopped when I was only thigh-deep in water.

"Where did you get those?" I asked, pointing.

His gaze had fixed on my breasts. His jaw worked, his tusks shifting across his upper lip.

"Kreel?"

"Uh . . ." He mumbled something I couldn't make out.

"Eyes on my face, Kreel," I said sternly.

He gulped and coasted his gaze slowly up to my face. Why did it feel like a caress?

"What did you say?" he asked.

"The markings on your arms and chest. Where did they come from?"

He looked down at his body and a shudder ripped through him. While he pawed at the marks, trying to rub them off, his gazed returned to mine. "They . . ."

I sat in the water, covering myself to my chin. I felt too exposed, too raw when he stared. It felt good, and that wasn't how I was supposed to feel with Kreel.

"They're what?" I asked. "Do they only show when you're wet?"

"You're wet?" he asked.

Actually, yes, in more ways than one, but I would never admit that to Kreel.

"No, I meant do the markings on your chest and arms only appear when *you're* wet?"

"Oh, these, um . . . no."

"Then why did they appear now?"

"I am not going to tell you."

# 11

## KREEL

Cora had sparked my awakening. Soon, I would fall into my lunar-long mating frenzy. I would crave her and *only her* for weeks. After that, I would cycle through my frenzy on a regular basis, and only she would be able to satisfy me.

She was my employee, here on a temporary basis. She would leave, and I could do nothing to stop her.

I hated this. Many of my people looked forward to meeting their fated ones. To their awakening and what followed. Not me.

I felt coerced into doing something I wasn't sure I wanted.

Then it occurred to me. I could fight it. That thought made my spine loosen. I would ignore her and the roar of need rising inside me. It would be easy. We'd finish my dwelling, and she'd leave. I'd slide out of my frenzy with no one but me aware.

She swam across the river, oblivious to what she'd

done. No, she hadn't done this. The fault was completely mine. My body had awakened to her alone, and I had no one to blame but myself.

When I sensed there was something different about her . . . When I'd watched her wiggling ass on the roof . . . When I'd started to desire her, I should've sent her away. Only then could I have stopped this.

If I avoided touching her, this would work out as it should. I couldn't claim her. She wouldn't want me, and as her beastly boss, it would be inappropriate for me to show interest.

Members of my own species would find me attractive, and I'd used that to my advantage in the past. I must appear repulsive to a human. I was twice her size, my skin was a different color, I had tusks, thumb claws, a tail, and horns. And my surly attitude would not win her friendship, let alone her undying affection.

Good. This would keep her away.

Comforted that I had a plan to keep my frenzy from achieving its full bloom, I relaxed and finished bathing while she paddled around, exclaiming over the vegetation lining the bank, the clearness of the water, and the joy of getting clean.

I turned away and tried to forget how gorgeous her body was when she stripped and strode toward me. Just that memory of her lush frame made my cock smack against my abdomen. The ripples encircling the thick length quivered. When I buried myself inside her, they'd vibrate her to orgasm.

I groaned and started swimming upriver as fast as I could.

"Where are you going?" she called out. "Can I come?"

*Come?* I barked out a growl.

There wasn't anything I wanted more than for her to come while I drove myself within her.

"Kreel?" she said again. "Where are you going?"

"Leave me alone."

She huffed and mumbled a few things I was glad I couldn't hear.

I swam harder, and as each stroke pulled me away from her, my awakening lessened. When I rounded a broad bend, I could no longer see or hear her. Only then did my flesh stop twitching. The markings were permanent, however.

They branded me as hers.

I scoffed. To think me, a mighty orc, would awaken for a puny human.

I didn't swim back to the bank until after she'd left the water and returned to my dwelling. By then, the sun had nearly slipped away for the night. Hopefully, she'd zipped herself inside my tent and wouldn't emerge until morning. I'd rise at dawn and get working on my house. The sooner we finished, the quicker she could leave.

Should I send her away?

I huffed. Damp and dressed, and without a cock poling within my pants, I felt confident I could resist her. I strode toward the house in complete surety. If the markings hadn't formed on my skin, I could tell myself I was mistaken, that Cora wasn't my mate.

Distance had helped. Finally, my cock had released and dropped back between my thighs. I was in control of this, not my body.

When I didn't see her near my dwelling, but I spied a light on inside my tent and the flap closed, I fully relaxed.

I tugged a few blankets from a chest inside my house and took them to the fire, throwing them near enough so the coals would keep me warm.

After chewing on an herb that kept my teeth and tusks from rotting, I lay on the blankets, staring at the flickering flames.

When I only saw her, I shoved the idea of her from my mind.

I could handle this. My awakening could be stopped before it finished lighting my mating frenzy.

I wouldn't beg her to fuck me.

# 12

## CORA

I woke early the next morning to banging. Not the kind of banging my body had craved all night as I breathed in Kreel's scent clinging to his blankets. I was out of my mind to think he'd want to do something like that with me.

No, I was out of my mind for dreaming about him shoving himself inside me from the front, behind, and sideways. In between those episodes, I dreamed of him pushing me against a wall and driving his thick cock within me to the hilt.

Groaning, I stretched and shoved off the offending blankets. I was horny. It was nothing more than that. And I sure didn't need a surly orc to take care of this simple matter.

Ditching my t-shirt, which I was heartily sick of wearing after sweating in it the day before, I started stroking my breasts. With my eyes closed, I glided my hand between my legs. Yes . . . Who needed a long, thick, ridged cock plunging inside? Not me. I could do this myself.

Panting, I stroked my clit, pushing my fingers inside my opening while pumping up my hips.

Because this was my fantasy, I could take it wherever I pleased. Right now, I lusted after Kreel—something I'd never share. There was no harm in pretending he was the one bringing me pleasure.

*Yes*. It felt so good.

"Like that, Kreel," I whispered.

My eyes rolled back in my head as my explosion loomed ahead.

My breathing echoed inside the tent, and I started rocking against my fingers faster, really getting into the pretend feel of his cock driving inside me.

Until the tent flap smacked open.

I ripped my eyelids apart and my fingers stopped moving, though they were still buried to the hilt inside me.

Kreel poked his head inside the tent. His eyes widened as his gaze took in my breasts with perky nipples, my legs spread wide and halted mid-thrust. My fingers buried inside my passage while my thumb remained frozen on my clit.

He groaned. His face darkened, and I swore the stripes on his upper arms and shoulders that had been gray last night turned black. That wasn't possible. Him being here wasn't possible. This was my space.

My orgasm.

As he gaped, saying nothing, I dropped my hips and

slid my fingers out of my wet body. They glistened, but I tucked them beneath me, as if that would make all this go away.

I'd lost the thrill, though it had been taken over by a new heat, one where he stepped inside, closed the tent flap, and dropped down beside me. He'd finish me off, then go for seconds. Thirds, because I'd totally let him.

My gaze was drawn to his pants. His cock shoved against the fabric, a stiff, thick rod I craved to feel pumping inside me.

What the hell was wrong with me? I wasn't here for sex. I'd leave soon and forget all about him.

I licked my lips, and he stared in fascination at the movement.

The spell between us broke.

"Get dressed," he growled, his gaze shooting to the tent ceiling. "It's past dawn. You need to work."

He stepped backward, and the tent flap dropped. His footsteps moved away—no, they *ran* away.

Fuck.

I scrambled out of bed, having no more interest in pleasuring myself. Sure, my body felt unfulfilled.

But I had a feeling it was going to take one specific orc to satisfy my needs.

I wanted to slink into the woods and hide. Flames kept climbing into my face. He'd caught me in the middle of my heat.

There was nothing wrong with taking care of business by myself, I kept repeating in my mind. Everybody did it. His mistake was not announcing his presence before thrusting himself inside my tent. His tent. Whatever.

I really needed to stop thinking about thrusting.

It was silly. So, he'd walked in while I was getting myself off—or about to do so. It meant nothing. He wouldn't say anything about it, and neither would I. I was here to do a job, as he'd so gruffly pointed out, and I'd do it. Then I'd leave and forget all about Kreel.

I nodded to confirm this idea and took the lift to the roof. Ignoring him working on the left side, I strode to the right, where he'd kindly laid two stacks of shingles.

A glance his way showed him leaning forward, his nicely muscled butt poking into the air. His hands kept busy snapping shingles together, aided by his enormous hammer. He wore no shirt, and the cords on his back rippled in the sunlight.

A droolworthy view right there.

His broad shoulders gleamed, misted with a light sweat and he had more dark tattoos coiling across and down his spine. I could swear they weren't there yesterday. I would've noticed something like that, right?

I studied his horns as he moved and wondered how they'd feel if I held onto them while his head was tucked between my thighs.

"Stop staring," he snarled, not looking up. "Get to work."

"Will do, Boss," I said, saluting him. The gesture came out snarky, but I was falling back on irritation to avoid thinking about him walking in on me. There was danger in all this, because I was beginning to like him despite his surly attitude.

"We'll continue until mid-afternoon, eat, and head into town," he added, still not glancing my way.

Oh, yeah, we had to get me something other than meat to eat and more clothing. The stuff I wore would be solid with sweat by the end of the day. I needed a comb and something other than my fingers to do my teeth. I'd used his bar of soap last night at the river, but it would be nice to have my own.

At least I wouldn't need to beg for pads or something like that.

Even better, no chance of making babies.

Making plans for what I'd do when I left here distracted me from my aching clit. I got to work, laying one shingle after another with my tiny-for-Kreel hammer. He continued slamming the shingles into place with his big one.

I really needed to stop reminding myself that everything about Kreel was big.

We worked well together, sweeping across the roof, passing each other with ease. Surely, he could see from my nicely laid shingles that I was an asset, not a bother.

As for his crankiness, that seemed to be pure Kreel. It

must've sunk into his skin while he was growing up, and he would be stuck with the attitude for life.

I could deal. Frankly, him acting snippy and pushing me away made this easier. I could pretend I hadn't almost gotten off while fantasizing about his cock.

We didn't stop until the sun started slumping toward the horizon. By then, I was famished and thirsty enough that I could drink the entire river.

"Done for the day," he said. Straightening, he flexed his body to the left and right, then back and forth. He bent forward to touch his toes.

I tried not to drool at the play of muscles across his body.

I had it bad. Tonight, when there was no chance he'd interrupt, I'd take care of things. Once I'd gotten off, I could relax and the sexual tension clouding around us would disappear.

I'd even avoid swimming in the river with him. We could take turns. No more stripping off our clothing and frolicking at the same time. We hadn't exactly frolicked, but we'd come close.

"Let's eat, and then we can go to the village." He walked down to the edge of the roof while I secured the rest of my pile of shingles. I studied the work I'd done in satisfaction while he jumped to the ground—show off.

We'd made considerable progress. Another day or two, and we'd finish the roof. Then we could start applying the siding.

Once the frame was buttoned up, we could work inside. At this rate, I'd be out of his hair—or whatever the white bands on his head were called—and gone from here within a month or so. An ambitious goal, but with the way my body craved his, I needed to keep that focus in mind. Thirty, forty days. I could handle that.

He retrieved the slabs of meat from inside the house, and I was grateful he'd warmed them before bringing them out. I could toss down a nice steak on most days, but I wouldn't enjoy it cold. For that, it needed cheese and bread. Salt and pepper. A salad.

He said nothing while he ate—and he purposefully placed his chair as far away from mine as he could.

"We leave," he said the second I'd dropped what was left of my hunk of meat on my plate and sighed with satisfaction. "I will harness the cart."

"I'll help," I said, standing.

"No!" He blinked, staring at me with a look I couldn't define. His gaze traveled down my front, and in one second, I was on fire again. If he crooked a claw, I'd trot over to him. He could rip off my pants, turn and bend me over the table, and . . . "Stop it!" he bellowed.

"What?" I licked the remnants of the salty meat off my lips.

"Do not look at me. Do not speak to me. And do not come near me."

"There's no need to shout. Jeez, are you always this hot and bothered?"

"I am not hot or bothered. You are . . ."

"I'm what?" I lifted my eyebrows, watching a variety of expressions cross his face. Irritation—that was a given. Impatience—ditto. But I spied heat in his eyes—I had to be mistaken.

He didn't want me that way, and that was how it needed to be. Dreaming about him fucking me was one thing. Inviting him into my—*his*—tent was a whole 'nother matter.

He strode around the building to hitch up the cart. Hitch it to what, I had no clue. I took the plates to the river and washed them. After, I lugged the bucket of meat inside and found a walk-in cold room where I could store it. The plates, I dropped into the wooden box holding cooking implements, though that was mostly knives.

Stepping outside, I smoothed my hair. I looked a wreck, but there was nothing I could do about it. I'd lift my chin and ignore the stares when we rode into town.

The shuffle of feet and a low huff made me lift my head.

Kreel sat on the bench mounted on the front of a wagon. The wagon was hitched to two matching, red-eyed beasts. When they saw me standing there, stunned, one stomped a hoof and flicked its spiked tail back and forth. With dark red hides, the beasts would tower over elephants, though I hadn't seen them other than pictures in books.

The creature on the right tipped up its long snout and shot fire toward the sky.

# 13
## KREEL

After gaping a few moments, Cora trotted over to the wagon.

"In the back," I barked. If she sat beside me, her raw, delicious scent would cloud around me during the entire trip. I would not be able to resist touching her, even in passing. And when I touched her, my awakening would grow stronger. I'd drag her into the back of the wagon and ravage her body.

I'd never force her, but from the scent of arousal clinging to her all day long, she wouldn't protest.

Why had I walked in on her when she lay inside my tent?

I'd pictured her slumbering, and that made my cock kick forward. Once I got control of that, I'd believed I could politely ask her to rise and join me on the roof.

Instead, I'd found her pleasuring herself.

For the rest of my days, I'd never forget the sensual joy on her face, her eyes half-closed with excitement. Her fingers teased her pert nipples. Her other hand was buried between her legs. I'd smelled her lust, so strong, I could almost taste it. I'd seen the gleam of her wetness on her fingers and between her thighs.

It had been all I could do not to rip off my clothing, push her hand aside, and plunder her body with my cock.

Despite my overwhelming urges, I was not a beast. I did not force females, and certainly not the one who appeared to be my fated mate.

"I can't ride up front with you?" she asked pertly, staring up at me with her lips twisted and humor-tinged irritation in her eyes.

"No."

"Why not?"

"I said no." I added a growl for good measure.

Her lips just quirked up. "Okay. I'll ride in the back like the hired help."

"You *are* the hired help."

"Come on," she said as she strode around to the back. "I thought we were starting to become friends." She climbed into the back of the wagon, but instead of sitting as far from me as possible, she crawled across the wooden boards and plunked her luscious ass on the floor right behind me.

I could smell her, and the heady, musky scent was going to drive me out of my mind.

"All the way to the back of the wagon," I said, a croak growling in my voice. "The back!" Because she was right, we were sort of friends, I added one word. "Please."

"Ah, so you do have manners," she said.

"I am an orc, as you so kindly pointed out. Orcs do not need to act in a polite manner."

"Then you fit your species to at T," she muttered as she crawled all the way to the back and rested her arm on the lifted gate. "How long does it take to get to town?"

"Not long." I lifted the reins and clicked my tongue to get the brutes moving. Playful, they danced about before settling down.

I growled when one shot fire again. I needed to exercise them more often.

Like many females, this one got flighty when she wasn't ridden hard and regularly.

They eventually settled and stopped their infernal prancing. At my shift of the reins, they started forward, pulling the wagon down the hill from my home. We reached the intersection at the bottom.

"Can you tell me about this place?" Cora asked, her voice alight with curiosity.

"This road," I pointed to the right and left, "encircles the main part of the village. Private residences built in the hills like mine connect to this road. At four places, like the spokes of a wheel, more roads lead to the center of town."

"How many live at this colony?"

"Hundreds."

"All kinds of species?"

"Exclusively Ulorns."

I caught her frown. "I haven't heard of them."

"They are a quiet species."

Her laugh snorted out. "Something you must enjoy."

Mostly. "I try to . . ." I stiffened my spine. "There are no other orcs here."

"Huh. Does that make you sad?" She crooked her head, watching me, but I kept my face neutral.

"Why would it?" I asked. She knew of my upbringing.

"Because . . . I don't know. There's no one else here like you?"

"I do not need friends or companions. This is a job, like any other, and it will prove I am worthy to my brethren."

"How will they know? You said you plan to remain here as long as you can."

"That is up to the elders."

"Who are they?"

"Stop chattering."

Her shoulders curled forward, and her face reddened. "Sorry."

Now I felt mean, and while I rarely cared what others thought of me, I didn't want this sole human female to be upset with me.

Even more, I hated to see her sad.

"You may sit up here with me," I grumbled reluctantly.

"Really?" Like a yarling, she scrambled across the floorboards and climbed onto the big bench, plunking down beside me. Our thighs brushed, and I stared down at them, marveling at how small she was compared to me.

How in the world had the fates decided this being

and I could mate? I'd crush her with my weight. My cock would split her in half. And my seed would flood her. Orcs were known for delivering buckets of cum.

Still, her scent. I breathed through my mouth, but that only activated my tastebuds. What would she have done this morning if I'd tugged her fingers out of her passage, licked them clean, then drove my tongue inside her?

"What are your . . . dragons called?" she asked, dragging my mind to the present.

I bit back a groan and tried to focus on my driving.

"I do not know this term dragon," I said. "These creatures are called culairs. They are indigenous to this planet."

"A dragon is a beast from human lore. They have long claws, tails with spikes, they fly, and they shoot fire from their throats. Like these beasties."

"Perhaps your lore comes from someone traveling and bringing tales of culairs to your planet?"

She shrugged. "Maybe. Are they tame?"

"Tame enough for me to hitch them to this wagon that they now pull into town."

"I assume these are adults."

"Of course. Their young are tiny."

She chuckled. "Tiny seems to be a relative term."

"If one catches a culair when they are small, it is possible to tame them."

"You haven't been here long enough to catch babies, so I assume you bought these big boys?"

"Only one is female."

"I'm not going to ask how you can tell."

"No balls. No cock."

Her gaze shot to my groin, and heat swam through me, heady and overwhelming. My cock didn't need much when Cora was around. It slammed against my pants, straining the seams.

She gulped and dragged her gaze to the culairs. "You, um, didn't buy them."

"I caught them grown and tamed them."

"Really?" she breathed.

My chest puffed, though I didn't like how she could make my pride shine with her simple admiration. "It was not that difficult. They listen when I speak."

"They're huge."

"So am I."

She laid her hand on my arm, and my skin twitched. Flames licked through my markings. When they matured, they'd release a chemical inside me that would make my body produce more cum. It would also drive my hunger to a fever pitch—the frenzy, we called it.

I would crave mating for a full lunar cycle.

My body would not be satisfied until my fated mate carried my young.

# 14

## CORA

When his skin twitched under my fingers, and dark flames appeared to lick along his tattoos, I snatched my hand away.

"Sorry. I shouldn't touch you without your permission."

"You can . . ." He stiffened and turned to face forward, his greenish-blue face darkening. "You are correct. Do not touch me unless I beg."

"What?" The word barked out.

"Without permission," I said. "Do not touch without permission."

"You said beg," I mumbled, and frankly, part of me wanted to beg him. What was going on with me? It was like this guy emitted pheromones. My body sucked them in and slammed them into my clit. I ached down there, which wasn't right. My clit throbbed like I'd been stroking it for hours without the blessing of a release.

"Do not think things like this," he said.

"You have no way of knowing what I'm thinking."

He turned, one side of his thick brow rising. "No?" His attention drifted down my front, and I swore my nipples went hard solely from his gaze. What would it be like if he touched them?

Humans didn't go into heat, but it sure felt like I was teetering on the edge. "Maybe I'm the one who should be asking you not to touch without permission."

He snorted, his nostrils flaring. "If I touch you, you will enjoy it."

"Cocky, aren't you? What happened to your orders?" I deepened my voice, mimicking his earlier tone. "Do not look at me. Do not speak to me. And do not come near me?"

"Those rules still apply."

"Then tell that thing between your legs to stop smacking against your pants unless you plan to do something serious about it." I was joking about the last bit. Mostly.

Shit, I *was*! He was my boss. My grouchy boss.

Yeah, that didn't matter much, either. I found his snarls sexy. Each time he snapped at me; my clit twitched.

Kreel wrapped the reins around his hand. He clicked his tongue and tapped the leather straps on the backs of the culairs. They picked up their pace to a jarring trot, and the wagon clanked behind them, the vibration hitching up my spine.

We raced toward town, me clinging to the side of the wagon.

I decide to cut back on the heated talk and thoughts —the latter providing quite a challenge to avoid. It wouldn't go over well with the villagers if they caught me groping Kreel.

A few nicely built, brightly colored buildings started peppering the side of the road, each with vegetable gardens and window boxes with blooms. Shade trees gave a cozy feel, and a few animals lowed behind the buildings.

Two children rushed out the front door of one of the buildings as we passed. Slender and with deep burnished skin, they had tiny horns jutting from their black hair, and four arms, two legs. One pointed and giggled, and I assumed they laughed at the culairs who did have a somewhat comical appearance.

Until Kreel stiffened and color flooded his face.

As we grew closer to the main part of town, the buildings had been built almost on top of each other. A wide street traversed the center.

More kids and a few adults came out to watch us pass.

"I take it these are the Ulorn residents of the colony?" I asked in a low voice. I sent one a glare, but they just stared back, their gaze dismissing me to lock on Kreel again.

"Yes."

Someone snickered behind us, and the laugh was followed by others. Many pointed.

Kreel's spine tightened further.

They were *mocking* him.

A vise wedged my heart, and my eyes watered. How dare they?

Fury crashed through me; a storm ready to rip the world apart. My spine ramrodded, and I leaned close to him, wishing there was some way I could send him reassurance.

His lips remained a slash on his face, and he kept his gaze trained on the culairs. His hands twitched on the reins.

It crushed me when his shoulders curled slightly forward.

Leaning around him, I glared at those watching. Spying my florid face, a few eased back inside their houses. Parents dragged their kids away.

My breathing had gone ragged. "Fuckin' suckers," I bellowed. "Mind your own freakin' business!"

The last of those gawking, pointing, slunk away.

Kreel looked down at me and for one second, I swore I saw affection in his gaze.

# 15
## KREEL

I couldn't believe it. Cora defended me. This tiny human being who'd sparked my awakening defended *me*.

Like I was someone worthy of protecting.

No one had ever done something like this for me. Not a former orphan. Never my leader. And certainly not his mate, who doted on her yarlings alone.

When I found the stone that led me to the mine, I rejoiced, because it gave me a chance to escape my disheartening life. But even credits couldn't make my life complete. No, I needed the approval of my clan. I was not a useless orphan.

I was Kreelevar Nohmal Trirag Grikohr, and I would prove myself worthy.

It was only because I'd been in the right place at the right time that I'd gotten this position. When I heard it offered to my clan, I'd begged the leader to give me this chance. I'd needed hope for a solid future. A reason to lift my chin and take pride in myself.

Since I was the town manager, the residents obeyed my rules, but I doubted any of them would ever say they liked me. Respected? One of the elders, perhaps. And those they'd elected as intermediaries who'd worked with me to plan what shops we'd allow and where the residences would go.

None of them had made an effort to carry on more than a limited conversation with me and only then, about business. Always business. Never telling me to have a good day or asking if I was lonely up on my hill.

Lonely, me? I scoffed. I wasn't. Not truly.

But Cora sparked a dream I should toss aside forever, that of a warm home and a loving female to greet me at the end of a hard day.

"Why did you do that?" I asked, keeping my voice even. Too often, I barked, or my words came out gruff and angry. It was reflex, left over from when I was young.

"Do what?"

"Defend me?" Her action kicked me in the chest like the clawed hoof of a wily culair. I couldn't catch my breath.

My markings flared, blazing before settling to a deep, dark black. Heat poured into my groin, and if it was still this morning and Cora lay on my bed with her legs pumping up to meet her fingers, I'd be unable to resist storming inside and claiming her.

Something I could never do. She might be my true

mate, but this female would never want me, not like my body and my soul was beginning to want her.

I was huge. An orc, as she so politely pointed out.

I was not worthy of this tiny human female.

"Because they're assholes," she grumbled. "How dare they act like that with you?"

"Their actions mean nothing." My hands shook where they held the reins. What she'd done was everything but nothing. I wasn't sure I'd ever get over it.

"I'm sorry." Her hand dropped onto my arm and squeezed. "I understand what it's like to have very little, to feel like you're only the subject of mockery."

"I have always been worth something," I said, stiffening. I wasn't irritated with her—a new feeling for me. "Let this go."

Her hand snapped back, and she held it against her belly. "All right. Would you rather I didn't speak up for you?"

I got the feeling she'd be angry if I held her back.

"I appreciate your gesture, but it was unnecessary."

Her face cratered, though I didn't want her sympathy. "I'm sorry."

"Sorry, sorry, sorry. Why say such a thing? I never liked this word." She wasn't responsible. She couldn't fix what happened in my past.

"Then I won't use it again." Her words came out stoic, resigned.

Why did this make my hearts clench tight? I pushed the question aside.

"My father was an orc like me, but my mother was of

another species, one called the Suline. From her, I got this." I pointed to my tail. "Orcs do not have tails."

"Well, you do."

I grunted, agreeing with her. "Just as the Ulorns laugh here, I was mocked for this when I was a yarling."

"It's mean."

"I quickly learned to ignore it."

She tapped my chest. "I bet you couldn't ignore it inside here."

"In my hearts?"

"You have two?"

"Doesn't everyone?" I grumbled.

"I have one."

So deficient. "What if your solitary heart fails?"

"Then we die unless we can get a mechanical replacement."

Hmm. "I will overlook your deficiency."

Her lips twisted. "Thanks. Do you remember your parents? They must've loved you."

"I was too young when they died."

"You mentioned your leader raised you?"

"It is common for a clan leader to take in those without parents. With war often raging, there were many of us."

"But you weren't one big family."

I stared forward as I guided the culairs through town. "I was always apart, partly due to this." I pointed again to my tail. "I was different, and my people do not like anything out of the norm. I've had to work harder to prove myself."

And my chance came with this colony.

"People were mean to you your entire life?" She sounded sad. I was tempted to hug her.

An odd thought. I hugged no one.

"It didn't matter," I said.

"Well, it matters to me."

I didn't ask her why. Instead, I urged the culairs close to the rail mounted on the walkway spanning the front of the store. As the colony grew, others would open larger centers of commerce, but for now, this was the only one.

While a few of the townspeople gawked from the wooden sidewalk, we climbed down from the wagon.

In other colonies, the residents preferred technology. Hovercars, completely mechanized homes, and even robotic beings to do all the work. This colony was formed with the goal of a simple life. The Ulorns worked their crops and built what they needed. They walked rather than rode in computerized vehicles.

Wagons, of course, were permitted, as were taming beasts of burden.

I didn't come into town often. Only when I had great need. Even then, I purchased my items quickly and went to my office to handle disputes and manage land assignments for new settlers. I never walked through town without a purpose, and I only came to the store when I couldn't find what I needed on my property.

Fortunately, the settlers watching us from the walkway didn't snicker or point. Gawking I'd almost become used to.

Cora sent them a lifted eyebrow, and they backed away, putting distance between us as we stepped up onto the walk and strode inside the store.

"I only need a few things," she said. "As you said, you'll take them from my salary."

Her shuttle transfer here alone would eat up much of the credits she'd make just helping me finish my home. But she stared up at me with a hint of how I'd felt as a yarling, gazing with longing through windows at items for sale I'd never be able to afford.

"Of course," I said. "Get what you need." I'd saved almost everything I earned from my mine, putting it away for a future I could barely dream of. One could not take credits to the grave. I had plenty to share with Cora.

She strolled around, tugging clothing out from racks to hold up against her body, frowning as she noted each top had sleeves for four arms.

I went up to the counter. The Ulorn female standing behind the wooden barrier gave me a soft dip of her head. While she presented a polite façade, her deep blue eyes remained flinty. It was only after I'd arrived here and started building my home that I learned the Ulorns had demanded one of their own be chosen as manager of the colony. Their request had been denied.

"I need a tent," I said.

"We do not have any."

"*When* will you have them?"

"I do not know."

My growl slipped out. "All right. I need fruit. Vegetables."

"What kind of fruit?" she asked sullenly. "What kind of vegetables? How many? I will need more information before I can fill your order."

I was only half paying attention to her, instead watching Cora out of the corner of my eye. She held up a pale green dress, something one of the Ulorn females might wear. Totally inappropriate for a construction assistant.

Cora must've agreed because she returned it to the rack. Her gaze lingered on it as she moved away, however, and I couldn't miss the longing in her pretty eyes. She straightened her shoulders and turned to a rack containing pants and shirts, the correct clothing for her position.

Where would she wear a dress like that?

For some reason, I could picture it draping across her lush frame. Her smile as she twirled, the skirt flaring around her legs.

One of the locals would give her a leer as he made plans to seduce her.

My growl ripped through the room.

The Ulorn female at the counter backed away, her four hands lifting. "I . . . will. Fruit. Vegetables. Plenty. A wide variety. We have no meat, however."

"You're vegetarian?" Cora asked.

The Ulorn frowned. "Meat is too difficult to come by."

"I understand," Cora said in a sunny voice. "I can't imagine strolling into the woods to hunt."

"We do not have all day for conversation," I said dryly.

"I will fetch your purchases right away, sir!" The Ulorn female scurried into the room behind the counter, and the door banged closed behind her.

As I paced in front of the counter, Cora strolled ahead of me, leaving her light, heady scent behind. The scent made my cock twitch. I could barely stand it. How was I going to spend the next lunar cycle working beside her without throwing her to the ground and ravaging her? A male Thoksas in his full awakening had a voracious sexual appetite. He'd rut with his mate for weeks, his body determined to impregnate her.

Cora would never stand for something like that, and despite my brutish manner, I was not cruel. I did not force females, and nothing would induce me to push Cora into doing something she did not desire.

The Ulorn female returned carrying two boxes loaded with fruits and vegetables. Could anyone consume that much food? I could, though I couldn't imagine eating more than one bite of fruit or vegetables every few suns.

Cora was tiny and would not consume much. It would rot.

"That is too much," I barked, not irritated with the Ulorn. More with my cock that demanded rutting. And with Cora for having such an appealing scent. I was finding it a challenge to resist claiming her considering I'd only met her the day before.

I would hold myself back. When she left, my markings would fade. I'd no longer crave her.

"Don't be mean," Cora whispered from beside me. She smiled at the Ulorn female. "Everything looks lovely. We'll take both boxes."

The female's spine loosened, and though she shot me a glare, her gaze softened when she looked upon Cora.

I understood why she behaved this way.

Everything but my cock softened when I gazed at Cora myself. My hearts . . .? I didn't want to consider what them beating in unison meant.

"Will this be all?" the female asked.

"I need these too," Cora said, laying two pairs of pants and two shirts with shortened sleeves on the wooden surface. "Do you have pins or something I can use to keep the extra sleeves from dangling?"

"I can take the shirts out back and remove the sleeves and close the holes, if you would like," the female offered with a hesitant smile. "You are new here?"

"I am. I'm Cora." She jutted her hand toward the other female, hooking her head in my direction. "I'm working for this grumpy dude."

I grumbled and huffed, but I couldn't stop staring at her. Watching her. Everything about her tugged me close and refused to let go.

Leaning sideways, Cora rested her head on my arm, gazing up at me with sparkling eyes. She teased, and I liked it. Too much. "Kreel may put on a rough front, but he's a marshmallow inside."

Hold on.

The Ulorn female tapped Cora's hand. "I am Bree-lair." Her smile twitched when she looked my way. "What is a marsh-mellow?"

"If you toast it over the fire, it's crusty on the outside but it still stays melty and yummy on the inside."

What was I supposed to think of that? "I am not melty, and I am *not* yummy."

"That remains to be seen," Cora said, sharing a smile with Breelair.

Which remained to be seen, me being melty or yummy? I didn't need to know. I didn't want to know.

I was lying to myself.

I stomped my feet and grumbled some more, unsure what to make of how she behaved. I was crusty, definitely. But that went all the way through. No matter what she said, I was not melty and yummy inside.

Part of me wished Cora truly believed this, however.

No. Wait. I didn't wish for this. I would work with her, but I would not let her steal my hearts, assuming such a thing was possible.

"This is an intriguing notion, something I had not considered," Breelair said, her wide eyes taking in my full frame. I felt as if she was looking at me for the first time. "You are truly working with *him*?"

"Sure. He's a great boss," Cora said. "Kind and patient, and he's . . ." Her lips quivered. "He's a lot of fun in the evening."

Breelair's eyes widened further. "Ah. All right." She swallowed as her gaze shot to me again. "If you would like to wait, Cora, I will alter your shirts. It won't take long."

"Is there a place where we could get something to eat while you're doing that?" Cora asked. "A drink?"

"The bakery has a few tables," Breelair said.

Cora's eyes lit up. "Bakery? Please tell me they make cookies."

Breelair frowned. "Bread. Aircorn, the head baker, bakes bread. I do not know this . . . crew-kees."

"You have no idea what you're missing, but I guess finding cookies here would be too much to ask." She laid a hand on her brow. "Alas, I will find a way to survive."

Breelair and I shared a confused look.

"Yes, um," Breelair said, gathering up the clothing. "If you wait, I will bring your purchases to you there."

"That would be wonderful, right Kreel?" Cora asked. "We can get a snack, maybe some tea or something like that."

I wondered how she had not only gained control of this situation but warmed Breelair's heart. I'd been here more than a lunar cycle and hadn't learned more than a few of the villager's names.

Perhaps I needed to put on a pretend, friendly demeanor, something a bit like Cora's—though without the *alas*—and introduce myself more often. Strike up a conversation. Attempt not to scowl.

There may be hope these people would come to accept me.

I did not wish to move to another colony to earn my honor, assuming I would be allowed to do so. If I was sent away from here, I might have to slink back to my planet and hide inside my empty mine.

I thrust out my hand to Breelair. "I am Kreelevar Nohmal Trirag Grikohr."

"Yes, I . . . know," Breelair said. She gulped and tapped my hand. When I didn't bite it off, her posture loosened. "I am . . . pleased to meet you." She shot a brow-lifted glance Cora's way.

Cora just grinned like a proud parent.

I didn't want her in a parent relationship. My body had made it quite clear how I wanted her.

My mind would remain in control. I was determined about this.

"Let me take one of these boxes to the wagon, shall I?" Cora asked, sliding one into her arms.

"I will carry them both," I snarled.

Breelair's smile twitched, but she somehow kept it lifted, perhaps because her attention remained directed Cora's way.

"No worries," Cora said. "I've got it. Come on Kreel. Let's go get something to eat."

"We already ate," I growled at her back.

"Not something from a bakery," she called over her shoulder as she sashayed through the front door.

"I . . ." Somehow, I'd lost all control already.

Breelair watched me, saying nothing.

"She is a human," I said.

"I see." Breelair's body tensed, as if she expected me to grab hold of her, yank her close, and rip off her head.

My hearts sagged, though I wasn't sure why.

"Thank you," I said.

Breelair sucked in a breath. "Truly?"

"It is a polite thing to say after someone does a favor, is it not?" I huffed.

"Of course. It is." She darted a glance toward the door, and I suspected she hoped Cora would reappear and step between us.

"The dress she was looking at," I said.

"Dress?" Her arms laden with Cora's clothing, Breelair scooted toward the door leading to the back room.

"This one." I strode over to it and removed it from the rack before thrusting it across the counter, toward Breelair.

She took it from me with limp fingers.

"Could you . . . *please* alter it as well?" Being polite definitely wasn't easy. Life was so much easier when I could growl.

I was rewarded by Breelair's tentative smile. "Of course, sir. If you would like, I will place the package in your wagon."

"And brave the culairs?" They terrified the villagers, which stunned me. I'd tamed them. They wouldn't hurt a teetser.

Breelair's face colored. "I will take care, sir."

"Kreel," I said. "*Please,* call me Kreel?" I stressed the polite word that felt rusty on my tongue.

She sucked in a quick breath. "I see, um . . ."

With a nod to her, I strode from the shop, determined to tell Cora we would wait at the wagon, that we would not be procuring bakery goods, or the fates help me, tea.

When I stepped outside, however, I found her surrounded by Ulorn yarlings. They giggled and touched her hands and sides.

She gave me a smile that made my cock kick forward and my hearts slam against my ribcage.

# 16

## CORA

"Ah, there you are," I said, scooting around the kids and stepping up onto the wooden sidewalk beside Kreel. I hooked my hand through his arm. "Ready to get something to eat?"

"We ate already," he grumbled, his gaze focused on the children.

They gaped at him, but a stern look from me kept them from snickering. I'd had a little talk with them— bribed them with a song, actually, to behave. The song was silly, something a friend taught me when I was young, about moons and stars and leaves rustling in the breeze. They'd stared at me in fascination while I sang it.

"The kids want to meet you," I told Kreel.

"Why?" He scowled at me before turning his glare their way.

Three of them took a step backward, but the youngest of them all, Thala, who was only three, came forward. Tiny, she had a hard time stepping up onto the sidewalk, nearly toppling backward before Kreel caught her arm and righted her.

She gazed up, up, up at him, her jaw dropping.

"Big orc," she chirped.

"Thoksas," Kreel said, his tone softer and lighter than I'd heard before. "I am a mighty Thoksas."

"Too-sas," Thala said, her smile widening to reveal her little fangs. "Like Too-sas. Kreel."

"You do?" Kreel appeared completely bewildered.

"Do," Thala said. She held up her four arms. "Carry?"

"Where is your mother?" he asked.

She shrugged. "Workin'."

The other three came closer, though their wary expressions told me they'd bolt if Kreel so much as looked their way.

I reached to pick up Thala. "You don't have to—"

"It is no bother," Kreel said, sweeping the tiny Ulorn up and plunking her on his big shoulder.

She grabbed onto his horn. "Wee!"

Come to think of it, him carrying her might actually be better than a song.

The other kids came closer, crowding around Kreel.

"Me, me!" they cried.

I grinned up at him. "You're quite a popular guy, Kreel."

"I am not—"

Thala squealed and rocked her torso. "Fast. Go fast!"

"The bakery is that way," he said. The scowl on his face was softened by the gleam in his eyes. It couldn't be humor I saw there, could it? Kreel laughing was something I had to see, though I doubted it would ever be offered to me.

I followed as he strode down the walk, the other three children scampering around his legs, begging to be held too.

Stopping, Kreel scooped the smallest of them up and plunked him on the opposite shoulder from Thala. The little boy grabbed onto Kreel's other horn and squealed.

As for the other two, Kreel hefted them and raced down the walkway, his boots stomping on the wooden surface, the children's peals of laughter trailing behind him.

Grinning, I hurried after them.

We reached the end of the walk and he jumped off, landing on the dusty soil. He crossed to the other side of the road and leaped onto the sidewalk.

Two male Ulorn gaped after him as he passed. One had a hand on the hilt of a blade sheathed at his waist. I cringed, hoping he wouldn't pull it and plunge it into Kreel's back. When the children squealed with happiness again, the male sagged against a building, his head tilted.

"He's being nice," I told them with a scowl. "You might want to try it sometime."

Their jaws dropped, but I didn't hang around to see what else they might do. I scampered after Kreel, who'd stopped in front of the baker's shop. A yeasty aroma floating in the air made my belly rumble.

Kreel carefully lowered the children to the walkway and stooped down to say something to them that made them laugh. He started to straighten, but Thala tugged on his pants. When he bent forward again, she kissed him on the cheek.

As they raced away, laughing, he blinked at me. His fingers lingered where Thala had kissed him, and I wanted to give him a big hug. I felt bad that his gruff demeanor kept everyone from seeing the soft, squishy, nice guy he hid inside. Kids could tell if you were a good person, and all they'd needed was a little introduction to Kreel. He'd revealed his marshmallow interior.

"Snack?" I asked, linking my arm through his. This made it easier to tug him through the door and inside. If I didn't drag him, I had a feeling he'd stay outside or run back to the wagon.

He followed, his grumbles rumbling around him, but he didn't pull away.

I dragged him up to the counter, noting the few tables with delicate chairs along one wall.

"What would you like?" I asked Kreel.

He glared at the glass display. "There is no choice. They have bread or bread."

"Please tell me you don't hate carbs."

"What is a carb?"

"Bread."

He huffed. "I do eat bread on occasion."

The proprietor who must be Aircorn watched us with bulging eyes, most of his attention focused on Kreel.

"Could I . . ." Aircorn gulped, his head tipping back so he could meet Kreel's gaze. "Could I help you?"

"We'd love a loaf of that long, crusty bread," I pointed, "and butter if you have it."

"We do," Aircorn said, and I got the impression he was relieved I did the talking. He leaned close to me, but his words were not spoken softly enough to keep Kreel from overhearing. "Are you safe? Do you need me to find a few males to help you escape?"

He thought Kreel had bad intentions? A ball of pain lodged in my chest. Why hadn't they seen the guy I did from the moment I met him?

Kreel remained stoic, but the light that had bloomed in his eyes when he carried the children faded.

I wanted to bite Aircorn's head off, but then he'd fear both of us.

I took Kreel's hand, linking our fingers, and leaned into his side. For extra measure, I batted my eyelashes at him. "Do you want anything but bread and butter, sweetie?"

Kreel frowned down at me. "What are you doing?"

*Jeez, play along, would ya?*

So much for pretending we were dating.

"Bread, butter?" I asked. "Anything else?"

"You are costing me more credits."

"I guess I am," I said, though I did feel bad about that. "Is it . . ." My face overheated. "I'm sorry. We don't need anything." I dragged him over to the entrance, where the hawk-eyed baker couldn't hear. "I don't want to take all your money. Can we . . . Can you afford—"

"Of course," Kreel barked. "I have more credits than you could ever dream of spending."

"It's okay for me to get a few things here, then?" I asked. "I don't want to burden you."

"Yes, get what you want," he growled.

He truly was cute when he was grumpy. Actually, he was always grumpy, which meant he was always cute.

"Have a seat, then," I said, relief making my throat spasm. "And I'll place our order. We can enjoy a snack while we wait for Breelair to alter my clothing."

Kreel's lips thinned, but he shuffled toward a table.

I hurried back to the counter and leaned over it, keeping my expression pleasant but making sure Aircorn heard my snarl. "You be nice to Kreel or else."

He scowled. "Excuse me?"

"He's a sweet guy, and if you're mean to him, you'll live to regret it." Though I wasn't exactly sure what I'd do to get revenge. In general, I wasn't a violent person. But I would not let these villagers deal any more shit Kreel's way. "He might be your boss—"

"He manages the village," Aircorn said in a snooty tone. "He is not our boss."

"You know what I'm saying. He's in charge here, but that doesn't mean he's not a person with feelings."

Aircorn shot Kreel a confused look.

"Be pleasant," I said. "And I'll . . ."

"What?"

I scrambled to figure out what I could offer. I doubted a song would work. Maybe if I could bribe him to be kind, he and all the other villagers would let down their guard long enough for Kreel to relax. Then they'd see the sweetie I'd already noticed. "I'll show you how to make cookies."

"What is a crew-kee?" he asked.

"Do you have sugar? Flour?"

"Flour, yes," he said. "As for sugar, its only use is to spark the yeast for my bread. Who would otherwise consume something like that?"

"Boy, are you missing out." I shook my head. "I want to buy whatever sugar you can spare, plus a good amount of flour. Can you also add a few flat pans to our order?"

"Why pans?"

"For baking the cookies."

He grumbled, but it was a baby grumble compared to Kreel's—and it wasn't cute at all. "I will add them."

"Perfect. Thanks."

Did Kreel have an oven?

I was about to find out.

# 17
## KREEL

I perched on the tiny, silly chair, worried it would collapse beneath me.

Cora, being her usual sunny slash irksome self, plunked a tray on the table and settled in the chair opposite mine.

I stared down at the floofy tea pot, two cups with saucers, plus a plate holding evenly cut slices of bread. A mound of pale creamy goo sweated on a small plate. I wasn't sure I dared touch the goo, let alone eat it.

"Yum," she said, rubbing her palms together. She shot me a grin. "I'm a carbaholic. I can't wait to fill my need."

My body suggested it had a solid idea about how to fill her needs. I needed to shut it down now. I couldn't walk around with an anaconda in my pants for the next lunar cycle.

Hopefully, I wouldn't have to. All I needed to do was stop my awakening and the mating frenzy that would follow. She would never know. I certainly wouldn't tell her how much I craved her flesh. She'd finish the job and leave, completely unaware of the danger she'd avoided.

"Tea?" Cora said, holding up the pot. "I'm not sure what herbs he included, but it smells delish."

I grunted.

She poured.

"I didn't think to ask for cream or sugar," she said. "Would you like either? I don't mind challenging Aircorn one more time to get them for you."

"No."

"I imagine you already know, but Aircorn's in competition with you."

What? Competition to claim this female? My growl ripped through the room, and I started to rise, knocking my thigh against the table, and sending everything on the flat surface rocking.

Cora latched onto the tray to keep it from falling, then grabbed my arm, nudging me back into my seat. "Slow down there."

"Competition?" I roared.

Her eyes widened, but humor sparkled there. "Just competition for being the grumpiest guy in town. That's you. Grump extraordinaire."

Ah, so she was not attracted to the baker. I had no reason to feel jealousy. She was not mine. She would never be my mate. I would never fuck her. She could fuck the world for all I cared.

Her smile widened. "You really did get up on the wrong side of the bed this morning, didn't you?"

"I did not get up on any side of a bed. I did not sleep in my bed, because *you* were in my bed." Pleasuring herself. It was all I could do to back away and not stay to watch. My cock jerked upright at the idea, tenting my pants forward and smacking against the underside of the table.

Pinching my eyes closed, I told it to go away. Come back later. Maybe in a full lunar cycle, after Cora had left.

Suppressive thoughts weren't working.

At least she couldn't see it.

"Aw, you gave up your bed when you don't have another?" she asked, taking a slice of bread and coating it with a thick layer of the creamy yellow glop. She placed the slice on my plate and slid it closer to me.

Aircorn watched us intently, his scowl rivaling mine. I shot him a glare, but he just huffed and began wiping down the counter with a rag.

"I am comfortable sleeping on the ground," I said.

"Outside?"

"Where else?"

"Why not inside your new home? I know the roof isn't completed, but the outer walls will provide protection."

I hefted my arm, showing off my muscles. "I protect myself. Without windows and doors, it is the same as lying outside."

"I suppose." A frown formed on her brow, adding tiny creases to her beautiful face. "You *could* sleep inside the tent with me."

"That would be on the ground still."

She wiggled her eyebrows, a grin fleeting across her lips. "Unless you're inviting yourself to my bed."

Aircorn leaned forward, his ears lifting to catch every word.

"We will discuss this later," I said. No one would say a thing if I slept in the same tent with this female. That did not mean I wanted them to know what I did on my hill.

"All right. Joking is over." She tapped the side of my plate. "Eat." Lifting a second slice of bread, she coated it with more creamy slop. She took a bite and closed her eyes as she chewed, wiggling in her seat.

My cock slammed against the table again. Damn thing was trying to control me. My markings, too, that flamed beneath my skin.

I'd heard they spread pheromones to induce my potential mate to crave me. As she wasn't an orc, I doubted they had any effect on Cora.

They were driving me out of my mind from the inside out.

I raked my finger along one of the lines on my arm, but it wouldn't go away.

"You never did tell me how those tattoos could appear just by jumping into the water," she said, pointing at one with her slice of bread.

To avoid having to speak of this, I stuffed the entire slice into my mouth and chewed. Flavors exploded on my tongue.

"This is amazing," I growled. Crumbs rained down on my lap, and for one tick, my cock backed down to rest against my thigh. "The creamy slime? It is exquisite. I could easily eat this for every meal."

"Yay," she said. "We'll bring lots of loaves home."

"Wait, no. Meat," I grunted. "Orcs—*Thoksas*—almost exclusively eat meat. They don't consume . . . curbs."

"Carbs and why not?"

"Because this is how it is done."

"If you jumped out of your stiff, grumpy suit for a second, you might find it fun out here."

Would any of my brethren know if I added a bit of bread to my diet?

I grumbled, though truly, my hearts weren't fully into the sound. I did it out of principle to show her I didn't relent easily.

She smiled, wiggling as she ate the rest of her bread. After, she stared longingly at the last slice on the plate.

I nudged my hand toward it. "Take it."

"You're way bigger than me. You eat it."

"Eat it!"

"Aw," she cooed. "I'm feelin' the love right now." She scooped up the slice and covered it with the last of the creamy gunk, then consumed it in a few bites.

I drained my tea, grimacing at the flavor, and stood. The second her teacup hit her saucer, I grabbed the tray and brought it to Aircorn.

"I want bread," I told him.

Cora sashayed over to stand beside me. "We'd like to order some bread," she said in a pleasant voice. "We'll pay well to have it delivered to Kreel's house every few days, along with a crock of butter." She peered up at me. "Two loaves each time?"

"Four."

"Even better."

The baker sputtered, but we settled on a fee.

"You'll bring the things we discussed in our first delivery?" Cora asked.

She was going to drain too many credits before she was gone, but I couldn't drum up any irritation about it.

Who could care about credits when Cora smiled my way?

# 18

## CORA

When we returned to the wagon, we climbed onto the bench. Breelair had left the package with my garments in the back.

Kreel jiggled the reins, guiding the culairs from the village.

As the wagon jostled along, our thighs rubbed together. Kreel stared straight ahead, and I got the idea he was doing his best to ignore me.

I couldn't stop shooting looks at him from beneath my lashes. Against my better judgment, I was starting to like Kreel, though I wasn't sure what could come from it.

Sure, my body was hot for him, but I didn't need to sleep with him to satisfy that itch. I could do it myself.

Liking could turn into more, and that would not be a wise move on my part.

One, he was my boss.

Two, I'd leave here once this job was done.

Three, I didn't want to get hurt. I doubted he'd be attracted to me, let alone want anything other than sex. So me falling in love with him would leave me with a shredded heart.

Four . . . There wasn't a four—yet—though I was sure I could dream one up.

The best thing I could do was build a big wall around my heart and focus on helping him build his house. No touching hands. No leaning into his side. No getting caught playing with my clit while fantasizing about his cock.

Easy.

With that settled, I peered around as the culairs took us up the long slope leading to Kreel's home. Dark purple trees with paler purple leaves spotted both sides of the dirt road, interspersed with golden leafed bushes. Tall, lavender grass grew between the bushes and the road.

Once my mind got used to how different this was from Earth, I liked it.

"Are there other wild creatures living near the colony?" I asked. "Dangerous ones we need to watch out for?"

Kreel clicked his tongue and jiggled the reins, making the culairs pick up their pace to a bone-jarring trot.

"Kreel?" I prompted. Our thighs continued to rub together and frankly; the friction created heat that shot straight to my clit. What was it with this orc?

*One, two, three, four. Remember the issues related to those numbers.*

That was why I tried to focus on the area around us, the perfect distraction.

"Like wild cats or boars?" I asked.

He sent a look my way that made electricity zing up my spine.

"Me," he growled. "I am the most dangerous creature in the area. You must watch out for me."

So much for our sort of truce.

I said nothing after that, unsure how to interpret his words. If I didn't know better, I'd think he was interested in me. If he was, he'd do things to show it. He wouldn't grump and snarl. He wouldn't snap and act like he abhorred me most of the time.

Well, unless he was as scared as me of being hurt.

Now that was something to ponder.

To play it safe, I eased away from him until I perched on the edge of the bench, leaning against the wooden rail. When our thighs no longer rubbed, I could avoid thinking about other parts of us rubbing harder.

Faster.

My growl slipped out, and he shot me a confused look. I did not explain.

We reached his house and unloaded our purchases, placing anything we didn't want animals getting into inside wooden totes within the house.

"Back to work," he said.

As we laid the rest of the roof shingles, I thought about his comment, wondering what it meant. I hadn't come to any decisions by the time we finished and took our equipment to the ground.

"I'm going to the river," he snapped, not looking my way. "Do not join me."

"I'm stinky too."

He shot me an odd look. "You smell amazing."

What? Stunned, I stared after him as he stalked away, adding his comment to his earlier statement. Pieces of the puzzle were dropping from the sky, but they didn't make up a full picture.

I placed my package of clothing inside the tent, opening it only enough to remove a few clean items to wear after I'd bathed.

When he'd finished at the river, I grabbed the bar of soap we'd also bought from Breelair, a scrap of material I could use as a towel, and my clean clothes. I headed to the river.

Clean, I walked back up the hill, finding Kreel setting up a meal on the table. More slabs of meat sizzled over the fire, but he'd added a loaf of bread and butter from the baker, plus one piece of fruit and one stalk of vegetable, lonely things sitting in the middle of the table.

"What can I do to help get ready?" I asked.

"Sit," he said, not looking my way.

Nodding slowly, I took my place at the table.

When the meat was done, he plunked a loaded plate in front of me. To his own heaping plate, he added half the loaf of bread and a big scoop of butter.

Then he turned and stalked into the waning light, leaving me alone at the table.

"Where are you going?" I called after him.

He said nothing.

With a sigh, I ate my dinner and took care of the leftovers and dishes after. Since I doubted Kreel wanted to sit by the fire and sing campfire rounds, I went to bed.

Of course, I dreamed about Kreel all night.

# 19
## KREEL

"We will work on the exterior walls," I said. "We will not talk, and we will not touch."

I'd laid awake most of the night with my cock on fire. By morning, I'd solidified my determination to avoid Cora.

She gazed up at me, a frown storming across her brow. "Why can't we talk? I mean, I don't have an airborne disease."

"You do," I snarled in her face.

Her eyes swam, and she blinked fast. I was overcome with the urge to . . . hug her.

"I don't do hugs," I said in a softer tone. I didn't like making her sad. She brought joy to my life with her smiles and teasing. It was wrong of me to slam my boot on her happiness.

"I guess that's good, because I won't be asking for a hug," she said, her nose in the air

Good. She was backing away. That was for the best.

We worked on the siding, snapping the composite pieces together and securing it from the top down. By the end of the day, we'd finished one wall.

"You do fine work," I said when we stood back to assess our progress.

She huffed and crossed her arms on her chest. "Thanks."

"I mean it."

Her nod was a jerk of her head. "I'm going to bathe. Please give me privacy."

I struggled not to sigh as she gathered her things and walked down the hill to the river. This was how it needed to be. If she realized how much I craved her, she'd tell me to stay away.

If she knew how I was starting to care, she'd run in the opposite direction. Who could blame her? I was an orc, twice her size, and I had nothing to offer someone as lovely as she.

While she was gone, I started the fire. I'd have to hunt tomorrow since we were nearly out of meat.

I took my turn at the river when she'd finished, returning to find her sitting at the table with a big smile on her face. She pointed to a loaded plate in the center of the table. "Sit. Eat. Enjoy. The last only if you're capable of feeling joy. I'm not so sure about that."

It was a decent dig. I could appreciate her effort.

"I can feel joy," I grumbled as I tossed my dirty clothing into the tub near the house. Someone came from town every few days and took it, returning my clean things by the end of that day. Eventually, I'd wash my items inside my house.

"I'm not sure I believe you," she said, staring down at her plate. Her shoulders drooped. Was she tired? "As far as I can tell, you're a big lump of irritation."

"Just know I'm not," I said softly. I sat, not eager to explain why I snapped and snarled all the time. Even being this close to her made my markings flare. Soon, they'd turn blacker than night. They'd emit pheromones she'd have no idea how to handle, assuming it was possible for a human to feel them. In all likelihood, her body would ignore them while I'd salivate near her with a cock so hard, I could drill through stone with it.

That's when I realized I might have to send her away before my house was finished. When my body entered the final stage of the awakening, it would be too late.

I couldn't bear to scare or harm her.

She watched me while I dished up a hearty serving of whatever she'd made.

"Add this," she said, showing me by drizzling a pale purple sauce on the circular fluffy things that vaguely resembled the inside of bread. "It's not maple, but it should taste good."

"What did you make?" I was desperate to establish a normal connection between us, though I didn't want to analyze why.

"Pancakes. I also ground up some meat and added spices, fried it, and we can call it sausages." She pointed to peculiar lumps lying on the plate between us.

"You say they were originally meat?" I asked, stabbing one with my knife.

"If you don't like them, don't eat them." The glare she shot my way would've pierced my flesh if it had been sharper.

"They are meat. I eat meat." I lifted one and popped it into my mouth whole. My groan of pleasure slipped out while I chewed, and it was all I could do not to wiggle like she'd done with the bread when we sat at Aircorn's bakery.

She watched me; her eyes wide but guarded. When she slid her tongue across her top lip, I groaned louder.

"Don't do that," she said.

"Do what?" I truly had no idea what she was speaking of.

"Moan like you're about to come."

"If I come, you will know it. Orcs are known for the quantities we release."

"I should be grossed out by that comment," she snarled. "It should completely put me off my meal."

"Why aren't you . . . goosed out?"

Her head tilted, and she looked at me as if she wasn't sure why I'd asked. I truly wanted to know. She wasn't repulsed by the thought of profuse orc cum? Of course, now that I'd mentioned it, I could picture it filling her completely after I'd slammed into her for a while. When I pulled out, my seed would coat the inside of her thighs. It would drip down her legs when she stood, as it did for all orc females after they had sex.

"Cum is cum," she said. "Even if we . . ." Her face

pinkened. "I've got this." She slapped her upper arm. When I frowned, she explained. "I have an implant. I can't get pregnant."

"Would you ever wish to be pregnant?"

"Someday, maybe. I'd like to give a child what was stolen from me."

"Good parents."

"Yup, mine sucked, but don't toss me your pity." Her chin lifted. "I made friends, and they helped me get established. My home isn't palatial like yours." Her hand flicked in that direction. "It's a one-room apartment. But it's mine and I like it. I'll have to sell it when I get back, but I'll find something new. Better."

"Why will you sell?"

"Because . . ." Her attention fell to her plate. "Never mind. Try your pancakes. I'm curious to hear what you think."

I lifted one of the circular things coated with sauce and stuffed it into my mouth. It was even better than the spiced meat. Closing my eyes, I chewed and did nothing to hold back my groans. She'd heard them before. "This is wonderful," I said around the bite.

When I opened my eyes, I found her watching me with stark vulnerability on her face. It made me want to storm around the table, lift her into my arms, and hold her. Tell her life could be wonderful, something I'd never believed before.

Now, I wasn't sure. Perhaps, with Cora, life could be amazing.

I couldn't believe I was feeling mushy about another

being. I'd lived alone for many cycles, never believing I needed someone to make me feel complete.

With Cora, though? I worried once she left, it would be over for me. I'd solidify into a complete grump and never smile again.

She ate, and while there was nothing sensual about somebody chewing, my mouth went dry, and my markings overheated.

I needed to go jump in the river.

My cock sensed potential action and perked up, eager and hard within a tick. I didn't even bother trying to hide how it nudged against the underside of the table.

Her gaze fell to that area, and my cock responded, jerking some more.

"Does it always do that?" she asked, rising with her empty plate in hand.

"Ignore it." I ate more of the cake made in a pan, savoring the flavors. Then more of the meat. "Will you make this again?" Because she frowned, I added, "Please?"

"I want to do lots of cooking. That's the one thing I've enjoyed all these years. I rarely had ingredients, and I often had to improvise, but if nothing else, I make a mean cookie."

"I don't believe anything you make would be mean." Cora too. There was nothing but sweetness inside her. She cared, and that was the most powerful weapon in the world.

It had slayed me.

I lifted the empty plates and licked them, my long,

dual tongues gliding across the surface in opposite directions.

She stared at my mouth. "You have two tongues."

"I do. They are particularly long, as well." Perfect for cleaning off a plate.

More color rose in her face. "You really need to stop that."

"Stop what?" I dropped the plates back on the table.

Her eyes smoldered. I couldn't deny what I was seeing.

What if . . .? What if!

What if I offered myself to her, and she *didn't* turn me down?

# 20

## CORA

I'd barely returned from bathing in the river when the sky opened up overhead. Rain poured down as I raced for the house, joining Kreel inside the living room area overlooking the valley.

Fortunately, the rain slowed, though a chilly wind whipped through the open house.

"You're in the tent with me tonight," I said.

"Absolutely not."

He sounded resolute, but I could be stubborn too. "The tent."

"No," he growled. The tattoos on his arms darkened, if such a thing was possible. I still hadn't gotten an answer to my question of how he'd obtained them, and I had a feeling I never would. I could add that to my question of how they could darken before my eyes.

His nostrils flared, and I swore he scented me. He'd told me he was a dangerous beast, and I could see that, though I knew in my soul he'd never harm me.

Awareness flashed through me, and my body suddenly ached for his touch. I soaked through my panties in seconds, something that I'd only read about before.

I backed away from him, before the overwhelming urge to touch and lick him consumed me.

I couldn't forget his super long, spliced tongue. All I could think of was him placing it upon my flesh. Tonight, I'd dream about him gliding it between my legs.

He swallowed and took a step toward me.

I backed until my ass hit the framing between this room and the next.

*Get a grip, Cora!*

A slice of sun arched across the sky, striking the composite flooring.

"I guess you'll be fine outside after all. I'm going to bed," I said. Sleep was overrated. I was going to lie awake all night, writhing at the thought of his touch.

He grunted and pivoted, striding from the room.

"Okay," I whispered. "Goodnight to you too."

He was gone before the words left my mouth.

My lips twisted. Be that way. I used the facilities. After, I stomped to the tent and slipped inside. After stripping, I climbed beneath the blankets.

They smelled faintly of Kreel, and not in a stinky way. Contrary to what he might think, his scent was pleasant even after a day spent sweating in the sun. I might even say the aroma was arousing, which was silly. Sweat couldn't turn a woman on.

Although, when it coated a big, muscular frame and

gleamed in the sunshine? Let me lay on the ground and spread my legs wide.

I thought I'd lie awake all night, my body on fire, but I drifted to sleep.

I woke to rain drumming on the tent roof, cracks of thunder shaking the frame, and lightning flashing in the dark sky.

And a scratch on the tent flap.

Since I hadn't had time to pack a bag before I left, I only wore one of the shirts we'd picked up in town. No panties. I only had one pair. I washed them at the river and left them to dry inside the tent every night.

As for my bra . . . Who'd wear a bra to bed?

I scooted from beneath the blankets, yanked my shirt down to cover my ass, though the hem only came to mid-thigh, and padded to the door. I cracked it wide enough to peer through.

Kreel stood outside, wetter than a dog after a swim in the lake. All he needed to do was shake.

"I am sorry," he said, his thick bands of hair dripping, creating furrows on his naked chest and pooling at the top of his low-slung pants. "I . . ."

Jeez, how could I think with this tantalizing display in front of me?

"It's wet. You're wet," I said. "You're going to get me wet." Gulp. I already was, like this guy could hit a switch, and I'd pool between my legs for him. My brain did not need to go in that direction, however. "Come on." I parted the tent flaps and crooked my finger.

He stared at my hand for a long while before shouldering himself inside.

"There's plenty of room for two," I said, trying to sound businesslike. It was a complete failure. Even I could hear the huskiness in my voice. I'd thought I'd curbed my steamy thoughts when I left him in the house, but here they were again, moving in and setting up a full display for the bake sale.

I could be wrong, but it looked like ink bled through the lines on his arms and chest in sharp ripples.

He groaned, and my heart flipped.

My mouth went drier than bark.

"I will rest on the floor," he said, collapsing down beside the bed. "I will not disturb you."

"I could take the floor instead." Offering him a place beside me in his own bed would be a colossal mistake. There was no way I wouldn't be parting my legs, revealing I wore nothing beneath the shirt, and inviting him to plunder wherever his cock wanted to roam.

"No, I will take the floor," he snapped.

Good. If he kept his snarl in high gear, it would keep a wall between us.

"You can take at least one blanket." I tugged it off and handed it to him. "You should remove your wet pants."

"I will not."

I sighed. "They'll rub where you won't like it, but it's your balls and your ass. Who am I to tell you otherwise?"

Saying nothing, he rolled to face away from me, pulling the blanket up over his head.

Okay, grump. Be that way.

I dropped back onto the bed and tugged the remaining blanket up over me. Then I lay in silence, listening to his soft breathing, my body on fire.

I woke to a rattling and stared at the tent roof, wondering what was making the sound.

Rolling toward Kreel, I figured it out.

"You're freezing," I said softly. Would he hear?

"I am not."

"Your teeth are chattering. I bet your pants are still wet and your body's frozen."

"There is nothing to be done about it."

"Sure there is." Sliding out of the bed, I crawled close to him. I yanked the blanket from his under-the-chin clutch and reached for the fastening at the top of his pants.

He swatted at my hand, but his tap was like a baby's. "Leave me be."

"I'm trying to help. Take off your pants and at least then, your body will dry. You'll be warmer."

He rose to a sitting position that made him tower over me. "You are a pest."

"Yeah, and what else is new?" It stung that even after many days working together, he didn't have a single kind thought for me in his heart. "If you don't take your pants off, I'll do it for you."

His lips curled up, revealing how long his tusks were. "I dare you to try, puny human."

Who was I to skip out on a challenge like that? I tackled him, though honestly, his body barely shifted from my lunge. We wrangled a bit, me trying to reach for his pants, him evading my touch. His abs felt heavenly beneath my fingers, rippling rows of rock-hard muscle. Frankly, it was distracting.

My body started shaking with laughter, and he joined in, grinning down at me.

He toppled me backward, onto the tent floor, and loomed over me.

Still laughing, I scrambled to break the hold he had on my wrists with only one hand, his thighs straddling my hips.

My shirt had hiked up around my waist during my struggle.

His hand hit the bare skin of my belly. In his haste to yank it away, it dragged across the hair between my legs.

His fingers froze. He froze.

His gaze locked on mine, and he groaned, a hoarse cry of need and dismay.

As he lifted my pinned wrists over my head, he leaned down until his mouth hovered above mine.

"Tell me no," he barked.

There was no way in hell I could say that word because everything inside me shouted yes.

I shook my head and dared him with my eyes to claim me.

With a lusty growl, his mouth locked onto mine.

# 21

## KREEL

She wore nothing but a fucking shirt.
Nothing!

Only my crumbling will had kept my fingers from gliding down the slice between her legs, from wrenching my pants open and shoving myself inside her.

Her mouth, that sassy, snarky mouth that had begged me for a kiss from almost the moment I met her, opened to let my tongue inside.

My hand rested on her mound. I should snatch it away and lift myself off her. Leave this tent before I did something I regretted. I couldn't do that, though. My will to resist had fled, replaced by the roaring need of my full awakening.

My mating frenzy would consume me soon. Consume *her*.

She was fated for me, but I would never be able to claim her. I didn't want to claim her. She was a puny female human, a pain in my ass.

Yet I ached to possess her more than anything I'd ever craved before.

My cock jerked against my wet pants, a hot, stiff rod of need.

"Tell me no," I growled against her neck.

When she shook her head, I came undone.

My mouth crashed down on hers again, taking, then giving, my long, dual tongue gliding inside to tease hers.

I kept her hands pinned above her head, liking that I was in full control of this tick. A primal need rose inside me, telling me to fuck her hard. I wouldn't stop until she shrieked and quivered with pleasure.

But, despite my appearance, despite my orc blood, I would not force her.

When she arched her hips up, I couldn't resist. I carefully slid a finger down her slit.

A moaned worked its way up her throat.

Emboldened, I placed the blunted side of my thumb claw on her clit. I rubbed while she writhed beneath me.

I couldn't place a claw inside her. That would hurt.

But my tail would fit well. I coiled it up and glided it between her legs, stopping at her opening.

Lifting my head, I took in her swollen lips, her eyes heavy with desire. "Tell me no," I growled again, nudging the tip of my tail inside her.

She shook her head again. "I can't. I want . . ."

"I will fuck you with my tail unless you tell me not to."

All she did was give me a heady smile and hitch up her hips, her thighs spreading wider.

My hearts . . . banged together. There was no other way to describe it. Like I'd been frozen in a winter pond and spring suddenly arrived, something inside me melted. I couldn't analyze it. I didn't want to analyze it.

But I felt it. The feeling expanded within me despite my determination to ignore it.

I plunged my tail inside her.

Her gasp of pleasure rang out. Her eyelids shuttered as I moved my tail in a jerky motion. Out, then thrusting back within her. She was wet, oh, so wet, her body overcome with desire.

I stroked beneath her shirt, capturing her nipple with my fingers. When I rolled it, she moaned.

I shoved up her shirt and sucked the pearly bud into my mouth, nibbling at it with my tusks.

As I pumped my tail within her, and she met each thrust with a high-pitched cry, my cock demanded I fill her.

Doing so would solidify my awakening. My frenzy would take over, and I'd pummel her. I'd ram away until I dumped a huge load of cum within her.

That would hurt her—something I would rather die than do.

This situation couldn't go on, but for now, I would bring her pleasure. The morning would give me a solution, though I already knew in my hearts what it must be.

I moved my tail faster, sucking on her nipple while rubbing her clit with my thumb.

She exploded, her gasp echoing in the small space. Her sighs fed something inside me. Emotion? Nah.

Yet there it was.

I removed my tail from inside her, savoring the wet, sucking sound her body made.

Then I lifted her and crawled into my bed. With her tucked against my body and my blanket over us, I held her.

She slept while I struggled to put together the words I'd have to speak in the morning.

# 22

## CORA

I woke, alone in Kreel's bed. For a second, I thought I must've dreamed of riding his tail, of his mouth on my breast.

But when I rolled onto my back and stretched, the languid heat between my legs told me it had happened.

I'd nearly fucked my boss. Why hadn't he taken me? I would've let him. I'd wanted it more than anything. Even now, if he crawled back inside the tent and placed his fingers between my legs, I'd be moaning and writhing beneath him within seconds.

Fire roared across my skin. The heavy thud of my chest echoed around me.

I felt like I was in heat, something humans weren't capable of. But there it was.

I *craved* him.

After tugging on my pants, I left the tent.

I found him sitting at the table.

Hustling over, I tried to act casual. "I'll put out bread and butter for breakfast." Later, I'd take a break from construction and make my first treat. Something simple, maybe. Something that could be fried in a pan over the fire. I still hadn't determined if he had an oven.

"Sit," he barked. "Last night."

And there it was. I'd crossed a line, and he was going to tell me I needed to stay on the other side of the fence until it was time for me to leave.

Cringing, I sank down into the chair opposite him.

I couldn't meet his eyes. "I'm sorry. I shouldn't have tackled you or touched you. And I sure shouldn't have—"

"You have triggered my awakening."

I blinked fast, looking up. "What?"

"My awakening."

"I heard that part. I don't know what it means, however. You're . . . awake?" This made no sense.

"My body has awoken."

"Is that a Thoksas thing?"

He dipped his head forward. His tail stretched beneath the table. It coiled around my ankle, but the moment he realized what he was doing, he yanked it back. "My body will soon enter the mating frenzy, and you are to blame."

"Um, oh." I couldn't read anything from his stern face. Although, he almost always had a stern face. What would he look like if he gave me a true, heart-felt smile? I'd probably melt into a puddle if he did. My heart couldn't take it. "I'm sorry," I finally said. "I'll stay away from you. Will that help?"

"You must leave."

A band wrapped around my throat. "Leave?" Funny, when I contemplated leaving, I wasn't worried about the Vessars. Being chased by the lizard mafia was nothing compared to the thought of never seeing Kreel again. It shouldn't be like this. I'd only known him a few days.

But there it was. Last night had only solidified it for me.

"I don't know what to say," I said.

"I will arrange for transport."

"What will happen to you and your . . . mating frenzy?" A bitter taint crossed my tongue at the thought of him seeking out someone in town to take care of his needs. Would he and Breelair hook up?

Hell, maybe he'd choose Aircorn.

"I will . . . deal with it."

"Exactly what is the awakening?"

"Something triggered within an orc. A call to mate that persists for a full lunar cycle. This is when male bodies are fertile, and it only happens when we meet . . ." His gaze fell to the tattoos that had fascinated me from the moment I saw them.

Without thought, I ran my finger down the one on his forearm sitting on the table. Heat flared beneath my finger, and I hissed and pulled my hand back, cupping it while holding it against my chest. "What just happened?"

"You did this." He lifted his arm. When the sunlight hit the markings, they flared before settling down to a rich, inky black.

"Me? Not just anyone?"

His stern gaze met mine. "You caused my awakening. If you remain here much longer, my mating frenzy will fully trigger. I will not be able to leave you alone."

Hold on. "You're saying I sexually awoke you."

"Yes."

"And soon your body will wish to mate with mine."

"Yes."

I swallowed, shoving the lump down my throat. "Is this something you have control over?"

"If you remain here much longer, I will claim you. I will take you, fucking you until your body quakes around mine. I will not stop until I have filled you with cum to overflowing, and then my cock will wake again, and I will do this over and over until my frenzy has passed. For a full lunar cycle."

An entire month of hot and heavy sex, my body filled with his seed the entire time.

For some reason, the thought of that didn't repel me. I mean, he was a brute. He was grumpy, surly, and I should be running in the opposite direction.

Orc cum filling me to overflowing? It would drip down my legs. He'd take me from every direction. He'd do it over and over until I was a limp, orgasmic wreck.

I tilted my head. "Is there another option besides me leaving?"

He growled. "You are fired."

"Wait." I sagged, my shoulders curling forward. "You're letting me go, just like that?"

"Since you are fired, you can leave or . . ."

"Or what?"

"Remain behind and share my frenzy."

# 23
## KREEL

I expected her to leap up from the table and run all the way to town. To hide.

Instead, she stared at me, her mouth slightly ajar.

"You've fired me," she said.

That was all she could think to say? "Yes."

"That means you're no longer my boss. There's no more power dynamic between us. We're . . . equals."

I dipped my head forward, unsure where she was going with this.

I braced myself for the rejection I knew was coming. I'd laid it out for her, though I hadn't been completely honest. Yes, she'd triggered my awakening. Yes, I would soon be consumed by a mating frenzy. And yes, it would end within one moon.

The frenzy, however, not the awakening.

That would link me to her for the rest of my life. I'd always crave her. Only distance would keep my frenzy from rising each cycle.

When she licked her upper lip, it was all I could do not to groan.

"So, it's my choice to stay or leave," she said.

"It is not a choice," I bellowed. Birds shot from the tree, squawking. They fluttered into the sky, fleeing this area. "If you stay, I will claim you in a billion different ways during my frenzy."

"Whoa." Her breath whooshed out, and color rode high in her face. She fanned her cheeks.

"Go to my tent and decide. I will call for a shuttle if you have not reappeared within an hour. If your choice is to leave, I accept this. Remain inside the tent until the shuttle lands in front. You won't see me again. *I* won't see *you* again."

"Hmm." Her brow scrunched.

I pointed. "Go to my tent!"

Her eyes widened, but they also sparkled with humor. Seeing it not only irked me, but it also made my cock slam against the underside of the table.

"This is why you're aroused all the time." She swallowed and looked up at me. "I'm sorry. I didn't mean to do this."

"Go!"

Her lips thinned. "All right. All right." Rising, she glared down at me. "You sure are cranky."

"I am crankier now than I was when I met you."

"What a way to make a girl blush."

When I growled, she grinned. If my arms weren't pressing down on it, my cock would've lifted the table.

Turning, she hurried to the tent. I tried to read her

thoughts in how she moved, in how she shot a steady look at me over her shoulder, but I couldn't.

Grumbling, I rose, willing my cock to deflate. It ignored me, stabbing upward inside my pants. My frenzy had almost consumed me. I could feel it flaming through my blood, screaming I needed to take her.

I wouldn't do this without her consent.

After the way life had treated me, I didn't owe anyone anything, but I owed Cora the chance to make her own decisions.

I strode to the house, determined to put her from my mind and get to work. I sorted through the construction material, organizing it when it didn't need organization.

After carrying piles of siding and laying them on the ground in the area where I needed them, I paused, lifting the com encircling my arm.

My hearts thudding heavily, I hailed a shuttle. It would be here soon.

And when it left, Cora would go with it.

# 24
## CORA

What a decision. Truly, if I let my body make it, I'd be lying on the table right now with my legs splayed wide.

But a mating frenzy? An awakening? I'd never heard of anything like that before.

I got the idea he wasn't telling me everything, but I had no clue what he was holding back. I didn't know much of anything about the Thoksas, but this must be the norm on their planet.

I puttered around inside the tent, fixing the bed and straightening out his jumble of things. I found one of the shirts he'd worn before he ripped it over his head and tossed it off the roof, revealing his luscious muscles I would happily spend a day licking.

Would anyone judge me for lifting it and holding it against my face to sniff?

Grumbling, I dropped it to my thighs, though I didn't release it.

I didn't come here to sleep with my boss. Excuse me, my *ex*-boss. I came here to work, and now I no longer had a job.

He was clear, however. If I stayed, it would be because I wanted to be with him. He wasn't offering money—ick—and he hadn't done anything to me against my will.

I flopped back on the bed, still clutching his infernal shirt. Really, if I was going to leave, I should pack my things. Ha. What things? I only owned the clothing I'd arrived in, unless I counted the altered items we'd bought in town.

Sitting, I tugged the package up onto my lap and pulled each item out. The second shirt I'd selected, the other pair of pants, and underneath, something I didn't remember choosing.

Ah . . . The dress I'd admired but put back on the rack lay neatly folded in the bottom of the package. Breelair was a decent seamstress. She'd removed the lower arms and closed the openings so well; I wouldn't know they'd originally been there.

I smoothed the dress out on my lap. I wasn't a dressy kind of girl; jeans and t-shirts were my go-to clothing. But when I saw this, I'd pictured myself wearing it for Kreel. A silly, stupid dream I should've shoved aside the moment I had it.

He'd seen me admire it, and he'd bought it.

What did that say about the grumpy orc I was . . .

Oh, shit. I was falling for him, wasn't I? That wasn't

supposed to happen. He'd been my boss, not dating material.

What would happen if I put the dress on and emerged from the tent? If the shuttle was here, he might shove me inside and close the hatch. I got the feeling he wasn't happy I'd somehow sparked his awakening, that I'd also made his body start to fall into a mating frenzy.

My clit ached at the thought of what we'd done the night before. Had he been willing, or had I somehow forced him to do that with me?

Ugh, what a thought.

I needed to decide what I was going to do.

A dull thud outside told me the shuttle pod had arrived, and I was no closer to making my decision. I only had a few minutes before the craft would take off. I'd either be inside it, or I'd remain here.

I heaved out a sigh.

With resolution rising inside me, I got up and strode toward the tent flap.

# 25
## KREEL

I watched from the shadows inside my house while the shuttle landed. Bracing myself against an interior wall stud, I waited for Cora to stride from the tent. She wouldn't spare a glance this way. She'd step into the shuttle, the hatch would close, and the craft would leave. She wouldn't look back. She'd forget about me before the shuttle hit the outer atmosphere.

I was a fool. My hearts . . .

A growl ripped through me. I hadn't been completely honest with her. Yes, I wanted to spend my mating frenzy with her, but I hadn't told her everything she needed to know about the awakening.

I was afraid speaking the truth would make her want to leave.

Emotions weren't supposed to be a part of this. I'd let her believe I'd claim her for only a lunar cycle, then send her back to wherever she came from. I didn't tell her that by the time we'd finished, I would love her.

It wouldn't be forced; falling was part of the process. Since my frenzy was the only time that I was fertile, this ensured I'd remain with the mate who awakened me. It ensured survival of my species.

Me, love? I'd never believed that silly, crushing emotion would seize my hearts, but here I was, caring for her already and not only because of the awakening. I'd never wanted someone to be my everything.

She'd stirred me from the moment I met her. It was impossible for me not to love her. Not to crave her. I wanted to hold her up so she could touch the stars. Hand her every flower I could claw from the ground.

Give her my hearts that had been frozen inside me until I met *her*.

The tent flaps flipped to the side, and Cora hurried out.

Like I expected, she walked toward the waiting shuttle.

I cringed, barely daring to watch her step inside.

Then my guts dropped, as did my lower jaw.

She wore the dress I'd secretly bought for her. Why? And instead of climbing inside the shuttle, she walked around it.

"Kreel?" she asked, her voice lifted. "Where are you?"

Why did she pause? The shuttle wouldn't be here long. If she didn't get inside, it would leave without her.

"Can you come out?" she said. "Please?"

I read only sympathy in her voice, which told me she planned to say goodbye. That was why she'd donned the dress and called for me. She would wave, perhaps, push for a fake smile, and after that, she would leave me forever.

Could I bear that? I wasn't completely, utterly, over-whelmingly in love with her.

Not yet.

But my hearts already beat for her. Only when she left, when we put distance between us, would their patter slow. If I were lucky, she'd be gone before the frenzy fully consumed me. Then I could go back to snarling at the villagers when I was forced to enter town, and to finishing my house.

I'd return to my lonely existence.

No. I wasn't lonely. I was content being by myself.

Until Cora entered my life.

I felt stupid hiding inside my house. I should behave like other blooded orcs and stride out there with confidence solidifying my soul. Stand in front of her with my spine straight and my face smooth. Take her goodbye for what it was and allow her to leave without giving into my compelling urge to beg her to stay.

I swallowed the lump in my throat and left the shadows, emerging into the sunshine that highlighted her in all her splendor. The dress fit her well, hugging her breasts and accentuating her lush curves. Her legs jutted beneath, and while the females on my home world rarely showed their ankles, I admired Cora's. They were slender and defined, and I wondered if stroking her feet would give her pleasure.

Stopping a short distance away, I stared at her. I memorized the shape of her face and the way her hair was swept out by the breeze in a flag of sorts. Sunlight played with the strands, making them glow.

"I want to tell you my answer," she said softly. Her hands twitched at her sides and for a tick, I wondered if she was nervous. Why would she be? She wanted to leave. She'd forget me before she reached her destination.

Unable to speak, I could only nod.

"I'm going to stay with you," she said. Her lips curved up in a tight smile. She *was* nervous.

Hold on. What had she said?

"You're not leaving?" My voice croaked, and I hated that I sounded vulnerable, that my longing came through in my words.

"I'm going to stay here with you for as long as you need me." Her feet shuffled on the ground.

I stared at her as wonder filled me.

"You want me to fuck you?" I blurted out, feeling stupid the moment I spoke. Fuck was such a crude word.

An *orc* word. It was coarse and unrefined, like me.

Her laugh shot from her lungs. "Yeah, sure, I guess you *could* say it that way. I want you to *fuck* me."

While my mind and hearts floundered, my cock got the message loud and clear. It stiffened, shoving the front of my pants forward.

She took one step toward me before pausing.

I thought, yes, this is it. She'd change her mind. She'd announce that and turn . . .

She grabbed the hem of the dress and tugged it up

over her head, laying it aside with care. Straightening, she faced me, a slight smile teasing across her face.

"I assume you'd like to get right to the fucking?" she asked with a smirk I couldn't wait to kiss into a smile. I'd love this female fully. She would have no complaint. And when she screamed out her pleasure, it would be because *I'd* made it happen.

Heat roared through me.

With my awakening fully upon me, and my mating frenzy sinking into my bones, I rushed to her and swept her up into my arms.

I barreled into my tent, tugged the flaps closed with my tail and lowered her carefully onto the bed.

*My* bed.

With a growl, I crawled over her and captured her mouth with mine.

# 26

## CORA

What was I getting myself into? Actually, I was the one who was about to be gotten into. Haha.

With Kreel's mouth devouring mine, I soon lost all train of thought. All I could focus on was the feel of his mouth, the possessive growl rumbling in his chest, and the weight of his big body pressing down on top of me.

I was soon squirming beneath him, desperate to remove what was left of my clothing—his clothing. I needed to feel his skin rubbing against mine and now.

Should I fear all this? His appetite for food was voracious. I suspected it would be the same with sex.

But my body ached to be claimed. I needed to feel him driving inside me. A ferocious hunger rose inside me that had to match his. Nothing would satisfy me other than falling apart in Kreel's arms.

His tusks rubbed against my chin, but rather than causing pain, they felt good. He started tearing at my bra, his thumb claws making short work of the material. Shreds tumbled around us.

I shimmied out of my panties.

He braced himself over me, staring down at my naked form. Then he ripped away his own clothing, flinging it aside.

His fully naked, enormous form pressed down on me. He shoved his knee between my lower legs and pressed his cock between them, prodding my opening.

Then his breath caught.

With a shake of his head and a groan, he pulled his hips back. His mouth feathered down my neck, all the way to my breasts. His legs splayed on the sides of my thighs, freeing his hands to roam. He took care with his thumb claws, though the subtle drag of them felt amazing on my quivering flesh.

He cupped my breasts and stared at them reverently.

"You are perfect," he said.

Now was not the time to point out my flaws.

"So are you," I quipped, because he was. He might be big and greenish-blue and cranky too often. His tail may spike and sweep in agitation more than I liked. But all the pieces of him were perfect when smashed together.

He grumbled, but a vulnerable smile flashed across his face. "I'm too big. You're small. Perfect."

"This is perfection." I traced my palms across his shoulders and smoothed my fingers along his pecs. His tight abs got equal attention. I had to wiggle around a bit to reach lower. "And this." I ran a finger down his engorged cock. Beads the size of my pinky nail vibrated at my touch. "Ah. You come with enhancements."

His brow wedged together as he took in his cock. "This is me. I'm huge. Orcs are often this big or even bigger."

"I think what you've got is enough." More than enough. It was going to be a challenge to take him all, but I would do my best to bear it.

My grin rose. Yes, please, let me bear it.

"I mean these." I pressed on one of the beads and it moved faster beneath his skin, kind of gliding around in a circle. "This is wonderful. Put it inside me now."

His chuckle rang out, low, deep, and incredibly sexy. It might be the first time I heard it, but I suspected it wouldn't be the last. Once we crossed the line between friends to lovers, things would change. It would only get better.

"I am going to fuck you, but it is important to me that you are fully with me," he said.

"That's a switch from most guys." I waved to my body. "Get to it."

"You are demanding."

"So are you."

His smile rose, and it was lethal. He was making rings out of my emotions, and once he slid them onto his fingers, they'd never come off. After I'd had him, and him me, could I leave him?

I wasn't going to think of that. Now was the only thing that mattered.

Leaning over me, he kissed each of my breasts. Then

with a huffing rumble, he sucked a nipple into his mouth. His segmented tongue coiled around it and tugged.

My moan ripped from me, and I jerked my hips upward.

He shot me another grin, then kissed down my belly. This time, when he parted my thighs, he was gentle. I liked softness, but I also didn't mind a bit of roughness. I'd tell him later.

He kissed my mound and parted my crease. "Wet," he said, smacking his lips. "Get wetter."

"Yes, sir," I said with a laugh. "Coming right up."

"Yes, cum. I have lots of cum to give you. You will drip for days."

Why in all hell did that sound sexy? I should be cringing and demanding lots of pads. Instead, the thought of his slick wetness coating my insides only enhanced my fever.

He put his long, fantastic tongue to use, poking it up inside me. His tail coiled around his ass, and the tip latched onto my clit.

My brain shot through the roof and kept going. I was a gyrating, writhing mess in seconds, struggling to hold on while he licked and sucked at my insides.

"More," he demanded, gliding his tongue along one of his tusks. "I want it all."

I could feel my body gushing, preparing my passage for what would come next.

When he glided one of his horns inside me, I exploded, my body quivering with an orgasm. My vision blurred, and all I could focus on was the feel of that horn moving back and forth while his fingers teased my clit.

I shuddered and whimpered, overcome. To think we'd just gotten started, and we had the entire month to be together.

"I said I wanted more," Kreel said, pulling out his horn and grinning up at me. "But that was a good start."

A limp wreck already, all I could do was stare at him.

"Would you like to feel this?" he asked, rising up over me and centering his cock within my still trembling folds.

"Yes," I groaned.

He hitched my legs up on his sides, and with a forward thrust, he buried himself deep.

# 27
## KREEL

My focus had fled. All I could do was feel. Her tight sheath. How wet she was for me. The way her inner walls quivered and sucked at my cock.

"You are with me?" I asked, worried for a tick that I was hurting her. She felt so good, but she was incredibly snug. Her passage squeezed me, and I could barely hold back shooting my first load of cum inside her. If she said this was too much, I'd find a way to finish fast.

I didn't want to. I would ride her all day and night if she were with me. But one mention of pain or the need to stop, and I was done.

"More," she said, her hands feverish on my chest and sides.

When she pinched my nipples, I groaned. My cock shook, the beads coiling and spasming beneath the taut skin. They'd soon harden to add to her pleasure.

My enhancements. I wanted to roar with laughter and kiss her until all she could think of was me.

I started with a slow rhythm because she was incredibly tight. The stretch had to be almost too much. But when she lifted her hips up to meet me, and her eyes rolled back in her head, I pushed harder. Moved faster.

It was almost too much. The frenzy seized me and drove my actions.

"Yes," she cried.

I felt the first burst of precum coating her inner walls, making her even more slippery. It was my undoing. *She* was my undoing, my everlasting love. My fated mate. The only person who would make my life complete.

I was a gruff, burly orc. Barely able to carry on a refined conversation. But this female craved my tough.

She was my completeness, my other half.

As I plunged within her, the beads on my cock tightened.

She groaned. "More, more." Her frantic cries drove me on as I drove into her.

My balls rose, eager. My cock stiffened.

Hammering into her, I felt her inner walls start twitching. Her heady moan echoed inside the room.

With a groan, I came, shooting everything I had inside her.

# 28

## CORA

Fuck, fuck, fuck. I was well and truly fucked and not only between my legs.

How in the world was I going to leave this guy? It wasn't only about the sex, though that had been amazing.

He held me after, spooning me, stroking my hair, and essentially cooing. His cock remained inside me, jerking upward every other second, and he was right. I was already dripping.

Who would've thought taking on a boatload of cum would make me want more? It was dirty, right? But I guess I was dirty too because I wanted to get dirtier.

His fingers teased down my shoulders and paused at my breasts. When he rolled my nipple, an electric current shot to my clit. He must've felt my insides quiver because his other hand moved down between my legs. He glided his claw across my saturated clit.

The friction of his finger picked up pace, and I turned

into a moaning wreck, thrusting my hips back to drive his stiffening cock deeper.

"Up," he said, lifting me and plunking me onto my hands and knees. He moved around behind me. "Yes. Show me how wet you are, how eager you are."

I spread my legs, completely wanton. I already craved his driving force again. How was this possible? I should be sore and stuffing a towel between my legs to plug up the dam. Instead, I braced myself, arching my spine to make my ass stick up further.

He held my hips and centered his cock. A thrust, and he buried himself inside me. His groan seemed to make his cock tighten. It sure felt like it.

And those round things along his length. They vibrated and swirled, each stroking a different part of my inner walls as he began to move faster.

He leaned over me, one arm going around my waist not only to hold me up but to push me back as his cock drove forward. His other hand found my clit and that claw that had started this session glided through the wetness.

Need unlike any I'd felt before rose inside me. It was mirrored in my heart, and I wasn't sure what that meant. Emotions . . . they were grabbing hold of me despite my determination to resist.

The movement of his body drew me back to what was happening, how the feelings roaring through my body was feeding something I didn't want to define. Not yet. Maybe not ever.

There was no way to explain this. Emotions could

tangle you up and spit you out on the other side. You'd lay there, not knowing what in the world just happened.

I shook and trembled, crying out with each of his thrusts. Grateful his gritty sex gave me a focus outside my heart. 'Cause I wasn't ready to go there.

In no time, I fell apart again, my body clenching around his cock as he moved it faster inside me.

His growl was followed by another gush within me.

We collapsed on the bed, and while his weight should be too much, it felt heavenly.

His arms went around me, and his tail encircled my ankle, holding on like he worried I'd try to escape.

No way. He might be the one locked in a mating frenzy, but I was going to milk this for all I could for the next month.

And when I left, I had a feeling I'd be leaving my heart behind.

# 29
## KREEL

I filled her many times. Day passed into night, then day came back all over again. My frenzy had been tamed for now. It would rise again soon, however, and she would be waiting.

*Mine. All mine.* The feral side of me had been consumed by her. It had staked its claim, and it would not let her go.

My other side suggested caution. Would the feral part of me listen?

"All right, so," she said, smacking the bedding when my cock started to stiffen inside her again. All she had to do was move, and my body was ready. "Does starvation come with this frenzy package?"

"You wish to eat," I said. My own belly clenched, but my cock ruled everything. It would do so for a long time.

Even after the lunar cycle had passed, my body would crave Cora's.

Between yesterday and today, my will had turned to

mush. If she said sit, I would do it. Fetch, and I would collect whatever she needed. Surround her with everything beautiful? I would drain all my credits to do so.

*Eat.* Yes. She'd asked for food. This I could deliver.

I pulled out of her, and her body made a wet, sucking sound as it clung to my cock. It was all I could do to ignore the call. My balls quivered, saying yes, yes, they had more to offer.

Rising from the bed, I stared down at her luscious form. My cock smacked against my abs, making demands.

But my mate was hungry. A need to please her overrode my cock, telling my body to put aside its needs for one tick.

"Hey," she protested, her face buried in the mattress. "Um, where are you going? My belly can wait. Come back!"

Rocking back on my heels, I smiled to see my cum leaking out of her. Some would consider this crude. Actually, everyone but an orc would consider this crude.

But I took pleasure in the sight, because it revealed how well and truly fucked she was.

She was mine. No one and nothing were going to steal her away.

My possessive streak was rising to the surface. I couldn't deny it.

But this female was independent. She wouldn't bend to my will, and the last thing I wanted to do was force this and snap her.

I would make this work as it should. I'd satisfy my

frenzy and when it was finished, I would ensure my feral side didn't try to cling.

My hearts? Grumbling, I flipped the tent flaps to the side and stepped out into the bright morning.

My hearts could not be controlled any more than my frenzy.

With my cock bobbing against my abdomen, I strode into my home, where I collected meat—always meat to make my cum hearty—and a loaf of the bread, frowning to see it was the last. The baker would deliver more, thankfully, and I'd kiss Cora to show her how pleased I was that she'd thought of ordering it regularly.

Spying the other things she'd ordered, I walked over and studied them. I had no idea what to do with the pans. A meal was prepared over the fire, but I doubted these would fare well there. Perhaps they pertained to the preparation of vegetables? I would wait to see what Cora did with them.

After the lunar cycle.

She wasn't leaving the tent other than to bathe and use the facilities until then.

Sugar, the final package said. With a shrug, I juggled one of the small packets in my arms with everything else.

It didn't take long to get the fire started.

"Hey, what smells good?" Cora asked, poking her head from my tent.

"Lie down," I said pleasantly. "I will return soon and fuck you."

"I'm all for a guy doing the cooking, as long as he also does the dishes, but if you think you can keep me pinned inside the tent, even for stellar fucking, you have another think coming."

"I intend to pin you to my bed with my cock. That is the pinning you can expect."

"Cute." She stepped out of the tent with a blanket wrapped around her body. "You cook. I'm taking a bath."

As if I hadn't just told her what she needed to do, she sauntered down to the river. I hurried over to stand at the peak of the hill, watching as she tossed the blanket aside and splashed into the water, squealing with joy.

All right. She could leave the tent for bathing too. I would allow that because this view—

A sharp smell hit my sinuses, and I turned to find my meat scorching. With a huff, I yanked if off the fire.

Hearing her splashes and picturing the water gliding across her body made my cock rise for another idea.

I covered the meat and bread to keep it safe from insects, then I bolted toward the river.

# 30
## CORA

I f Kreel thought he could control me, he was about to learn a hefty lesson.

He could make my body melt and my pulse charge through the roof, but there would be balance between us. My mom had tried to run all over me when I was little, and I'd broken free. No way in hell was I going to allow Kreel to steal the independence I'd worked hard to establish.

He smacked his feet down to the shore. "I want you again," he growled.

"Uh, uh," I said with a grin, scrutinizing his body. "Your cock looks pretty limp to me."

His brow scrunched together, and his head jerked forward. He stared at his cock. "It *is* stiff." He sounded so bewildered; it was all I could do not to laugh.

But he needed to learn one lesson before we went any farther.

"Perhaps I can help it get stronger," I said, holding up my soap.

"That has fragrance."

"You have a skin condition that precludes applying scent to your skin?"

His frown deepened. "I do not believe so."

He was so much fun to tease. "Then trot into the water and let me get you to the point where your cock will hold up under action."

"I do not trot," he said. "I control all action."

He was so going to learn.

"Kreel." A warning came through in my voice. "Water. Soap. Stiffy. In that order only."

Grumbling in a way that made my heart patter, he stormed into the water and right up to me. "I am stiff already. Turn so I may use your body to show you."

"You say the sweetest things," I sighed. "Not. Turn around so I can wash your back."

"That will not make me stiffer. I promise, once I am inside you, you will be able to feel that it has enough erection to give you pleasure."

I was well aware of the lethal pleasure his cock could deliver. And my body was already rising to the occasion, my clit throbbing and my insides gushing.

Compromising, I swam around to his back and lathered my hands. I tucked the soap under my arm and stroked his back in long glides.

He groaned. "You are right. I am getting stiffer."

My laugh snorted out, but I cut it off fast. He was

incredibly cute with his gruff ways and his brutish belief that he was in charge of everything around him.

I moved my hands along his waist, and he groaned.

"Stiffer," he hissed. "Very much stiffer."

"I don't think you're stiff enough." Swimming to his front, I lathered my hands again. I nudged him backward until his cock emerged from the water. Veins stood out prominently along the surface, and I could see the beads humming. Yum.

I stroked his length with my soapy fingers.

His eyelids slid closed, and he thrust forward, meeting my hands. "I need to be inside you when I come."

"Oh, you will be."

After working him into my own version of a frenzy, and getting him groaning and quivering, I splashed water on his cock to eliminate the soap.

Then I bent forward and licked the tip.

His eyelids popped open. "What are you doing? A cock goes into a passage. No place else."

"Hasn't anyone sucked on you before?"

"Why would they do something like that?"

Oh, my gosh. "Allow me to show you."

I drew him inside my mouth, running my tongue down his length. He was too big for me to take all of, and I wondered all over again how this enormous thing could fit inside me. The stretch had felt amazing. I wanted to feel it again soon.

Moving my head, I milked him with my mouth.

Seeing how much pleasure he took from this turned

me on. My ass wiggled with need, and if I wasn't having so much fun licking him, I'd turn around and beg him to impale me.

He must've sensed my need because his tail glided down my spine. It centered itself at my core and stuffed a good part of the end inside me.

I moaned, the vibration passing from my mouth to his cock.

He turned into a frantic wreck, gasping and huffing as he thrust upward. His tail did the same, plunging into me over and over.

I was as eager as him. My moans made the small balls along his cock harden, and he moved faster.

His muscles tightened, and his balls bunched up tight. His fingers tightened on my hair, and his tail . . . It was all I could do to pay attention to what my mouth was doing.

"Yes," he cried, jerking his hips forward.

My body shuddered as I gave into my orgasm.

His quick grin showed he knew I'd found my pleasure, something I'd noticed about him quickly. Each time we'd been together, he'd waited for me to finish first.

While I wiggled against his tail, claiming everything I could from this orgasm, he fell apart. His groan echoed across the river. Grasping my head with both of his hands, he rocked forward and shot everything he had inside my throat.

I drank him down, and he was right. He did have lots of cum.

It tasted marvelous.

# 31
## KREEL

S o, I'd lost all control of this situation, but I wasn't complaining. What she'd done with her mouth . . .

"My cum belongs inside your passage," I said. "All of it." My words came out scolding, but everything inside me glowed.

She was turning me to mush, and I couldn't host enough energy to complain.

Would it be bad to soften? An odd thought. Orcs didn't do things like that. They ruled, especially in the bedroom.

I had a feeling it wouldn't be long before Cora completely ruled me. And by the fates, I didn't mind one bit.

My muscles had stopped quivering, and my cock had lost part of its stiffness.

An idea occurred to me, and I frowned. "You are right. My rod had not achieved its full potential."

She grinned up at me and licked the last creamy bit of me off her lips. "Sometimes, we all need a little help to bring things along."

"You will do that again sometime?"

"Anytime." Rising, she teased her palms across my chest. My abdomen muscles shook, and my cock started jerking upward.

She started bending forward again, but I stilled her.

"Not now," I said. "The next cum needs to be solidly seated within you."

"You love your cum."

I was beginning to believe I loved her even more than my cum.

She splashed backward, sinking into the water. "Go cook. I'm hungry."

It wasn't until I was halfway up the hill that I realized I hadn't even thought about arguing with her about who was in charge of all this.

Someone once told me I'd meet my fated one, and it would be over.

This person wasn't here to see it, but she'd been right.

---

"Oh, now this is interesting," Cora said. She sat at the table with the meal I'd prepared in front of her. She held up the bread. "What did you do to it?"

"I grilled it over the fire—"

"I like the smoky flavor."

"Then I laid a thick layer of the yellow goo on top. It melted."

"Butter," she said with a nod. "I love butter."

"And then I sprinkled it with the white crystal substance you obtained from the baker."

"Sugar." She blinked slowly. "You put sugar on the bread."

"I did." I dipped my head forward proudly. "I like it." I munched through the slice, savoring the thick crunch of this soogar between my teeth.

"I guess if we had cinnamon, this would work."

My body sagged. "You do not like it."

"Oh, no," she exclaimed. She took another bite and spoke around it. "It's yum."

I studied her face, waiting for sarcasm that did not come. "Good."

We ate, and while my frenzy still boiled beneath the surface, I needed to work on my house. With the rainy weather coming soon, I needed to finish applying the exterior walls.

We finished our meal, and I rose. "You will clean up from breakfast."

"Oh yeah?" She peered up at me, one eyebrow rising. I sensed a different sort of storm coming from Cora, though I did not know why. "Maybe I'm going to lounge in the river, and you can take care of the dishes."

"I will be working on my home."

"So will I."

"I fired you."

"You can't fire me," she said. "I'm here to do a job, and I'm going to do it."

"You . . ." I wasn't sure what to say to that. This female kept my mind scrambled and my cock on fire whenever she was near.

"But . . ." She dragged out the word. "Since you've asked so *nicely*," her eyes rolled, "and you prepared our breakfast, I'll clean up. But I'm warning you. Whenever I cook, you're cleaning up."

"Males do not perform this role."

"You're saying you threw away your dishes after each meal?"

She'd trapped me.

"No," I said reluctantly.

"In my life, males share the workload."

I huffed, confused about my whirling emotions. I wanted to please her in everything, yet roles had been established in my culture many cycles ago.

Cora was not an orc.

I craved her body and her smiles.

I was falling in love with her despite my wish to keep my hearts secure.

"All right," I snarled.

She danced around the table, humming a tune, and launched herself into my arms. "Thanks. You won't regret it."

I couldn't resist kissing her. I contemplated peeling off her clothing and bending her over the table, but I did need to work on my home.

"You distract me," I finally said.

"Ditto." With a nod, she started gathering up the dishes.

Sighing, I crossed to the building and lifted my hammer from where I'd left it leaning the day before.

"That's sure a big hammer," Cora said, leaving the dishes to come over to admire it. She traced her finger along the shaft.

My cock twitched, nothing new during a mating frenzy, though her touching my tool should not excite me.

"What other size hammer would I use?" I asked, hefting it. The metal end gleamed in the sunlight. "It strikes as it should."

Eyes wide and with her lips quivering, she nodded. "You're right. It strikes very well."

"It bangs objects whenever I need it to," I added, unsure where her humor came from.

"It sure does," she breathed, holding her arms against her belly. Her eyes sparkled, and bubbling sounds rose from her throat.

"Best of all, it can drive an object into a hole with one thrust."

Bending forward, she burst into laughter. "It . . . does all that and more. It is amazing. In fact, it's the biggest, bestest hammer I've experienced so far."

I frowned. "Why is this funny?"

"Oh, no, it's not funny," she said, still laughing. "I get it. It's a big hammer. It delivers all the blows you could wish for."

"I do not understand you." Grumbling, I stomped around her, heading for the pile of siding I needed to apply over the next two days.

"It's okay," she called after me. "I'm sure you'll find a way to drive that hammer at something soon."

# 32
## CORA

I was beginning to love Kreel's hammer. As I worked beside him over the next few days, I kept thinking about what we did inside his tent and at the river after we'd washed off sweat. I wanted to do it all the time, but we were busy. The rainy season would be here soon, and the house needed to be buttoned up to keep out the weather. Once we were working inside, we could take . . . breaks.

With the tight schedule, I hadn't had a chance to do any baking.

"Do you have an oven?" I asked as he held a wall panel up the right distance from the one previously mounted. I drove the fastener between them to secure it in place. My hammer wasn't as big as his, but it did the job.

"I do not."

"Hmm." I frowned. "I'd like to cook something

special for you, but it's easier to bake it than fry it over the fire."

"We could buy an oven," he said, his brow scrunching together. "It takes credits."

I held up my hand. "It's not a big deal. I don't want you spending money on something that's basically a whim for me."

"It would please you."

"Well, yeah, it would. But my thought is to please you."

"You already do each night in my tent."

And my body hummed at the thought of doing so again soon. "What I'd do isn't sexual."

He grunted and lifted another panel, nudging his chin to show he wanted me to fasten it in place.

My heart sunk. Making cookies wasn't necessary. I just kept picturing the look on his face when he tried them. He asked for so little, just sex and help building his house. He didn't have many possessions, seeming to enjoy living a simple life.

Cookies weren't much in the scheme of things.

"We will go to town after lunch," he said, lifting another panel. They spanned from the sill to the roof overhang, and I couldn't begin to budge them myself. He hefted them with ease, his muscles bulging. At this rate, we'd finish the outside of the building before lunch.

"Do you need more supplies?"

"That as well." He grunted. "I will need to hunt tomorrow."

"Can I go with you this time?" I was curious to view the beasts he'd regularly brought back for our meals.

"Why would you wish to do that?"

I shrugged. "Why not?"

"It will be dangerous."

I studied the woods behind the house where nothing appeared to move. "What's out there?"

"Many things. They creep and claw, and your skin is fragile."

"*You* hunt."

"We need to eat." He paused before lifting another panel, and his gaze drifted down my front. "I suppose, if you came with me, I could defend you."

"Gee, thanks."

He'd sounded so surly I couldn't hold back my laugh.

"Why are you always laughing when the situation and conversation contain no humor?" he asked, and I could tell he was truly puzzled.

"You're funny." I put my arm around his waist and leaned into his side. "Every day, you bring humor into my world."

"You are touching me. You wish for sex," he said, his eyelids hooding.

"I can touch you without it being sexual, right?"

"Of course." He sounded affronted.

"Because, sometimes, it's nice to stroke someone's arm or give them a hug, or I don't know, kiss them, without it having to mean they want sex. Intimacy isn't just about a cock pumping into a passage."

His head cocked, and I assumed he had no idea what

I was talking about. "All right. Then you don't wish for sex."

"I didn't say that exactly."

"What exactly are you saying?"

"That I want to be able to touch you without that always turning into an invitation to have sex."

"All right." He swallowed. "I just . . ." His gaze went to his cock pressing against the front of his pants.

Truly, his stamina was amazing. We'd had sex when we woke and after we did the dishes—that time getting both of us completely soaked when we rolled off the bank and into the water. I didn't know if his virility was pure Kreel or if this was Kreel with his hormones raging due to his mating frenzy.

As his fingers traced across my jaw and down to where the top of my shirt began, my body loosened. A low simmer began in my bones.

"This is not about sex," he murmured. "This is me touching you because it feels good."

My hormones shot through my brain. "I . . . I . . ." I'd made my point, and he got it. That meant I could turn this into something steamy, right? Women wouldn't come after me with pitchforks for standing up, then stepping backward. I hoped.

When his fingers wandered along the back of my neck, my moan slipped out.

"Tell me if you want sex," he said softly.

"I do."

He took my hammer from my limp fingers and

chucked it aside. "This is good, because I have a hammer that needs to do some pounding."

I snorted. "Now you understand why I was laughing about hammers the other day."

He gave me a true smile, and it made sparks fly through my veins. "My hammer always needs driving." With only a few slashes, he severed my clothing with his claws. The wisps of material dropped away, puddling at my feet.

"Hey, I only have one outfit left now," I protested, though my heart wasn't in it. My skin was on fire, and I ached between my legs.

"You can wear your dress."

"Not to build a house."

"It is easy to flip up, is it not?" He backed me toward the table. "Do not wear this slip of material beneath your clothing any longer."

With an odd reverence, he helped me remove my panties. He carefully set them on a chair.

"They're my only pair, but you could've slashed through those as well."

"I always get what I want, Cora," he growled against my throat. "But I will not harm your possessions. They are yours to do with as you will."

I shrugged. My underwear truly didn't matter.

I licked my lips and pawed at the fastener to his pants, undoing it. He shrugged them off, and his cock sprang free, eager and hard. He rarely wore a shirt, something I'd come to appreciate. Even his feet were bare. He used the short claws on each of his toes for purchase when climbing up the wall to secure the tops of the panels.

"Turn," he demanded.

He was still into control, and it was a battle we waged on a regular basis, both inside the bedroom and on the job. Most of the time, I didn't mind letting him rule what we did, because he always made my body hum.

"Unless you wish to face me," he said with great reluctance. He was learning I didn't always want to be dictated to.

"I don't mind turning." I did enjoy when he thrust into me from behind. He could go deeper, and his hands and tail could keep me on fire.

With a grin, his tusks flashing in the sunlight, he carefully pivoted me around. A few things remained on the table, and he swept them off with his arm. He lay me face down, then glided his fingers down my back. Reaching my thighs, he nudged them apart.

"Show me everything, mate," he growled. His tail coiled around my ankle, holding me as if he worried that I'd take flight. No chance of that. I wanted this and nothing was going to stand between us.

When my legs were spread wide, he licked my slit before burying his face between my thighs, his long, forked tongue devouring my clit.

I writhed and moaned as his tail slid inside me, moving fast and driving me to pure satisfaction.

When I was a gasping wreck, ready to scream loud enough to make the birds in the area take flight, he rose and braced himself over me. He had to lift my hips because he was so much taller, but his tail helped, wrapping around my waist.

"You want my cum," he growled in my ear. He grazed his tusks across my skin as I nodded. "Tell me."

"Give it to me," I moaned. "Now."

"Yes." One thrust, and he impaled me.

My body tensed before relaxing, quickly getting into the flow.

He moved within me, driving himself hard. *Hammering* me.

And when we came, we both growled.

# 33
## KREEL

After I'd taken her on the table, and then against the wall of my house, filling her with my cock and my cum, I retrieved her dress and gently helped her put it on.

I needed to stop cutting off the clothing I'd purchased for her. Or I could buy her hundreds of outfits in town and keep slicing. I loved the shocked expression she displayed when I did it, her gasps of protest that melted into aroused sighs.

She smoothed the fabric and grinned up at me. "I love this dress. Thank you for getting it for me."

Now I was the one who felt like singing. This female . . . It wasn't just the sweet way she responded to my touch or the way she teased me, though both of those made fire roar through my veins. She lovingly prepared my meals. She washed my back in the river. And I'd caught her mending a tear in my pants two days ago.

She didn't have to do these things. They weren't part of satisfying my mating frenzy.

Could she truly care?

I growled and clawed at the ground with my toes.

"We're back to that again, are we?" she said it in such a sunny voice, I knew I hadn't offended her.

"I have to go into town anyway. Gather what you need," I said, stomping around her. I wasn't angry with her.

I'd accepted that I might one day love her and then she would leave. It seemed acceptable until I truly fell in love.

I wanted to keep her after my frenzy waned. When she left, it was going to sever something deep within me.

"I'll help you hitch the culairs," Cora said in a cheery voice. She skipped to catch up to me as I strode around my house.

"I will do so. You could be hurt."

"By those fluffy things?" she half-sang.

"Culairs are scaly. They are not fluffy."

"I bet they're complete sweethearts."

She followed me to the big pen I'd built near the woods. Trees provided shade during the heat of the day, and the open area was filled with grass they could graze on. This breed also enjoyed meat, and I gave them part of each kill.

Cora climbed up onto the fence and swung her legs over to sit. "Look at them. They're so pretty."

I frowned at the culairs. One looked up and snorted, its red hide gleaming in the sunlight.

"They remind me of dragons," she said. "But without wings."

"If they could fly, they would kill us all." I opened the tall gate and stepped inside.

One of the beasts growled. I hadn't worked with them for days, preferring to work on my mating frenzy with Cora instead. If I didn't interact with them regularly, they could go feral. It usually took longer than a few days, but this pair was nesting. They had a clutch of eggs in a nest beneath the trees they would protect with their lives.

Cora tucked up her legs, her eyebrows lifting. "Be careful."

"They will not harm me," I said with bravado. Actually, they could, though I would not allow them to do so in front of Cora.

A breeze caught her hair, fluttering it around her, and I stood in place, gaping at how beautiful she was. She looked gorgeous in the dress I'd bought her, and her lovely face held a soft smile as she watched my every move. She was happy here. I'd satisfied her with the hammering I'd just delivered. There was nothing better than that.

Her eyes widened, and her hand lifted. "Watch out."

One of the culairs slammed into my back, thrusting me to my knees in the grass.

With a growl, I pivoted and leapt, landing on the creature's head. I grappled with the horns while it flung its head back and forth, trying to dislodge me.

Once I could get my claws on the ground, I could cling, then wrangle with the culair until it tired.

I expected Cora to jump off the fence and back away. Maybe run back to the house in terror.

I did not expect to find her creeping closer, her hand outstretched. She sang a silly song about flowers and birds, and I braced myself for the second culair to attack her while I was busy with the first.

The second did move closer to her, but it didn't snort or thrust its horns her way. While I gaped—and the culair I held onto stared as raptly—the second beast sniffed her outstretched fingers.

"There's a love," she cooed. "Aren't you a beauty?" Moving slowly, she approached its side. She glided her fingers down its neck. "Such scaly skin you have. You're amazing. A sorta tame dragon."

"They're not tame," I said as the culair I held onto jerked its head, dislodging me. I stumbled backward and fell on my ass.

"Sure they are," Cora said with a soft smile. "What are their names?"

"They do not have names." I got up and brushed off my pants, though I didn't really care if I was dirty. I only wanted to look good for Cora.

My sigh chugged out. If I was not careful, I would not only love her, but I would also let her stomp all over me. An orc male needed to remain in charge. He did not let a female rule.

If Cora wanted to stay after my frenzy faded,

however, would I be willing to compromise on something like that?

I growled, and the culairs stepped backward.

"Be nice and they'll act the same," Cora said. She wiggled between the creatures who stood twice her height. "I've always wanted to have a pet, but my mom wouldn't let me."

"They are not pets." I said it carefully, desperate not to stir the culairs. If they attacked her . . . I would not think of such a thing. "Step back."

She ignored me, patting the culairs and singing to them softly.

"Please," I added.

I wasn't used to anyone doing what they wanted despite my request to do something else.

Most of the townspeople scurried when I appeared, which was better than mockery.

When I pronounced a decision, the elder's head bowed, and they backed away.

This was the way things should be with an orc leader. If I'd learned nothing in the house where I grew up, I'd taken this lesson to heart. Our clan leader was strict in his lessons. Orc males needed to be strong. Ruthless.

Not limp vines, and especially not in front of a female.

Grabbing a harness from the where I'd hooked it over a fencepost, I strode back to the culairs.

Cora smiled and backed up to give me room. "They're beautiful."

"They are beasts I tamed to pull my wagon."

"They're sweet, and I'm going to give them names."

"You must not."

"You can't call them thing one and thing two."

I frowned, my hands stilling on a creature's head. "Why would I do such a thing?"

"It's . . ." She shook her head. "They need names."

"Then name them. It hardly matters."

"I think . . ." She tapped her chin. "Truffle and Poochie."

"These names sound ridiculous."

"What would you prefer?"

I stomped my feet, feeling as if I was being manipulated into something I wasn't certain I wanted. "Something masculine."

Her head tilted as she studied them. "Are they both males?"

"One is female."

"Good. She can be called Poochie. He can be called Truffle."

I could see I was going to lose this battle already. Names didn't make any difference. When she left, I would forget them.

When she left . . .

My hearts seized, and my frenzy started stirring again, insisting I show her she belonged to me because I could deliver amazing sex.

We had to go to town. We did not have time for such a thing. She dripped with my cum already, figuratively speaking. She'd stuffed a hunk of fabric up there after we finished, and I wasn't sure I liked that, but a male sometimes had to compromise on a few things.

I would pretend my cum leaked down her inner thighs—a universal source of pride for male orcs.

I did not need to fill her again until later.

"Come along," I told the culairs, tugging on the vines. They plodded behind me, cooperative.

"See?" I told Cora. "They just needed to be shown I am the boss."

One—Truffle—jerked his snout against my thigh, sending me sideways. I righted my feet and glared, but I swore the creature snickered.

Cora stroked his snout and he huffed and squeaked in his throat; a sound I'd only heard them make with each other. "You're the boss, Kreel. For sure."

I turned away before I could watch her laugh.

Once they were hitched to the wagon, we climbed up onto the bench. Cora leaned against my side, and I put my arm around her while shifting the reins to get the beasts moving.

It didn't take long to reach town. We passed many Ulorns, though none said a word. They watched Cora, and I couldn't blame them. It was all I could do to look away myself.

A few yarlings crept out onto the road and ran beside us. One started singing, taking up the song about birds and flowers Cora had used with the culairs.

She joined in; her pitch perfect to my orc ears. We didn't sing, but I could tell the sounds she made were lovely, because the Ulorns watching smiled and a few females shyly waved.

We reached the store, and I brought the culairs to a halt. Before I could assist her, Cora jumped to the ground. She climbed up onto the sidewalk and continued to hum and sway while I got down.

The culairs had decided they no longer wished to behave.

"Ask them nicely," Cora said from behind me as I snarled and tried to wrangle one of the heads close enough to secure the tie to the post.

"Nice will not make them do as I demand."

"Neither will being grumpy."

"I am not grumpy," I said with affront.

She burst out in laughter—again. A few yarlings nearby did as well, though they didn't point or appear to be laughing at me. No, they seemed to adore Cora and responded to her joy.

"Sure, you're not grumpy," she finally said.

"You didn't find me grumpy this morning," I said quietly.

Heat flared in her eyes. "That was because you'd nudged your head into an interesting location."

If we were alone, I would do it this moment, but the yarlings watched. Aircorn had come out of his bakery. He waved, though I was confident he did this for Cora, not me.

Even Breelair emerged from the store. She pinched the fabric of Cora's dress. "You look beautiful in this. The color!"

"I know," Cora said. "Isn't it perfect? I *love* this dress."

For whatever reason, my irritation fled, replaced with a growing need and not only for sex. My stupid hearts pinched, and only one of the culairs smacking me with a horn made me drag my gaze away from Cora.

"Get your head over here, Poochie," I said without thought.

The beast actually did as I asked, gently moving forward. I secured the tie to the post and turned to find Cora beaming.

"See? This is why they needed to have names."

# 34
## CORA

"And you will come to tea next week?" Breelair asked.

"I'd love to." Assuming I could get away. "We're busy with his house, though, so next week might not work. Maybe the week after that?" Once we'd made progress inside, we could take breaks.

Breelair kept shooting concerned looks Kreel's way. He stood near the entrance of the store, glaring at anyone who came near. Was he aware of how others perceived him? Maybe he'd decided if he could get people to reject him for his glare, he wouldn't have to put himself out there and be hurt if they rejected him for who he truly was inside.

But this couldn't continue. He needed this job. He wanted to prove himself. He was setting himself up for failure acting like this.

He'd hefted the solar oven onto his shoulders, something heavy enough I couldn't budge it when I tried.

"How do you bear it?" Breelair whispered.

"Bear what?" I asked. I gave him a silly smile and struggled not to laugh again. Whenever he was around, all I could do was grin. And moan when he touched me. During sex, I was too focused on him pumping or licking or stroking me to think of smiling.

"He's fearsome," she said. "He glowers and snarls, and he snaps his tusks at whoever comes near."

Not me, and I kinda liked that. He could be a beast to whoever he liked, but with me, he was gentle.

However . . .

"He's a pussycat," I said.

"Pussy . . ."

"Yeah, that."

"Is that his species? I thought he was Thoksas."

"Oh, pussycat is a teasing nickname." Which I needed to try on him. After all, I'd discovered I could make him purr.

"I see," she said. Her face smoothed. "You will finish building his house and move into town?"

"I'm supposed to return to Earth." My chest ached at the thought of leaving Kreel. He was so easy to love.

That thought stunned me, and I flailed my hands at my throat.

He must've thought Breelair was attacking or something because he growled and stepped toward us.

I waved, and he backed up to lean against the side of the door, his hawk-like gaze remaining on me.

Breelair scurried around behind the counter. I expected her to duck. "He can be . . . fierce."

I chuckled. "He is. He's strong and amazing. You should see him working on the house." I was gushing, but I couldn't help it. "He doesn't wear a shirt, and his muscles bulge. And when he gets sweaty—"

She'd gone silent.

Her mouth hung open. "You . . . You are attracted to him?"

"Sure. Why not?" I bristled, waiting for her to say something snide.

"Ah." Her posture loosened. She leaned across the counter and patted my arm. "Love arrives in the most unusual circumstances, doesn't it?"

"I don't love him."

Her low chuckle rang out. "It is all right. I understand. I am attracted to the baker."

"Aircorn's as grumpy as Kreel."

Her breath caught. "You are right. They are both grumpy." She peered at Kreel in a different way. "He is burly. This is good. And I believe he is also sexy with those muscles you described. Look at how he holds the oven so easily and how—"

"He's mine," I snapped.

Her golden lips curved up. "Yes, he is yours." She scampered back out from behind the counter. Leaning close to me, she dropped her voice to a whisper. "Aircorn is burly too. So many muscles in unusual places," she sighed. "Kneading bread is hard work."

I couldn't tell much about his body with him wearing a long apron.

"This is what I find sexy," she added. "His hips . . . And his—"

I placed a finger over her lips before she could say more. "Too much info, Breelair."

"Ah, yes." She grinned, and I couldn't help but smile back.

The last thing I wanted to picture was her and the baker going at it, but who was I to judge?

Kreel and I humped like rabbits whenever we could.

# 35
## KREEL

"It is time for me to go to my office," I told Cora as we left the store. "I will leave the oven in the wagon."

"Where's your office? I'll go with you." She peered left and right.

In the middle of town, the locals had built a fountain and encircled it with small gardens filled with stinky flowers. A few yarlings raced among the stubby trees that would take generations to fully grow. Some parents followed, watching their progeny benignly, while others sat on stone benches, reading or gazing around.

I couldn't understand the point of this area. Such wasted space. It could be used for commerce or dwellings, but the villagers had insisted.

Breelair followed us out of the store and onto the wooden walkway.

"Don't forget next week!" She tugged on Cora's sleeve. "And come back in a day or two for your new clothing." A frown brewed on her brow when she looked at me, but her face smoothed. She sucked in a breath and released it. "You, too, Kreel."

I nearly turned to see who she must be speaking to behind me, but there was no other Kreel in town.

Cora linked her arm through mine, another thing that stunned me. Why touch if she didn't want sex? We couldn't do that here, though I'd be tempted to climb into the back of the wagon. The sides were high enough to shield us unless someone directly looked.

She smiled up at me. "I think we can come back in a few days, right?"

When she peered at me with this adoring look, I'd agree to almost anything.

"Yes," I blindly said. The moment I did, I realized how foolish I would look to my orc clan. They'd chastise me for giving in to a female's lure, for allowing her to control my actions. "No."

Her smile thinned. "Which is it? Yes or no?"

Breelair watched us with a lifted brow ridge.

The village's two elders stepped up onto the covered walk and shuffled this way, leaning heavily on their intricately carved staffs.

Moonsten nodded to me as she passed. As the oldest of the pair, she would expect me to arrive at my office before or at the same time as them. She would not wait if I was not there.

My job hinged on working with the elders. This had been laid out in the contract.

"I need to leave," I told Cora. "You can remain here with Breelair or in the wagon."

"I'm taking a break," Breelair said, her gaze drifting to the bakery. "I'd love to visit some more, but I have other plans."

Cora grinned, her smile sweeping across me. "I understand."

I did not. Out of the corner of my eye, I watched as the elders left the walkway and started across the street. My office was halfway down the next block. They moved slowly and if I left now, I could arrive ahead of them.

"I have a meeting," I said, my voice tight with urgency.

"Who are you meeting?" Cora asked as Breelair hurried toward the bakery.

"The elders." I flicked my hand to where they plodded across the street.

"I'll go with you then. I'd love to meet them."

"No." The last thing I needed was her there. She would not remain silent if I asked, and she would butt in and mess things up.

"Why not?"

I growled, though my hearts weren't in it. She looked lovely in the sunlight, and I couldn't think of anything but getting her back to my house and plowing into her body. Then sitting by the fire and speaking with her. I might even ask her to sing, since I'd come to enjoy that.

She shrugged. "This isn't a hill I'm willing to die on." Her attention landed on the park. "I'll go wait on a bench for you."

That would do, except . . . "Do not speak with anyone."

Her sigh rang out. "This is getting old."

"Nothing has aged except me, because I am not going to make my meeting in time."

"Go," she said with a roll of her eyes. "I'll talk to whoever I please."

I grumbled, but short of looming over her while she sat in the park, there was nothing I could do.

She stepped off the walk and strolled toward the fountain.

I boiled with frustration but only for a short span of time before leaping along the walkway, nearly knocking an Ulorn female off the surface. Stopping, I grabbed her arm to save her, righting her position.

"You!" She smacked me with her bag, then stormed away from me, down the walk.

Another wonderful interaction with the locals. At this rate, I'd fail in my task and be sent back to my home planet in shame.

For a tick, my hearts clenched. I wanted to succeed here more than anything. It was my chance to prove to my orc people that I had worth. It appeared that, no matter what I did, I was going to fail.

The elders. I could dwell on my dwindling future later.

I raced down the rest of the walk and leapt onto the road. A beast of burden being driven by a farmer was coming this way. The creature reared back, shrieking. With the farmer's curses chasing me, I bounded across the road and up onto the next walk.

I arrived at the door to my office at the same time as the elders.

Moonsten grunted. The second elder, Yarleer, gave me a dark stare that gave away nothing.

"Thank you for coming," I said, drumming up social niceties Cora would use. She was always polite and friendly.

Yarleer grunted, and I realized how a surly attitude might be perceived by others. Was this how everyone saw me?

Shoving the notion aside, I unlocked the door with a swipe of my thumb on the panel, marveling at how so many things were rustic here while other things high-tech. The elders were quite strict about what technology they allowed. They wanted a community who lived as naturally as possible, but they were also not willing to give up the comforts they'd enjoyed elsewhere.

Opening the panel wide, I started to stride inside before realizing it might be politer to let them enter ahead of me.

"Please," I said, nodding to the two chairs in front of my desk.

Yarleer's jaw dropped. He stared at me like he'd never seen me before.

Moonsten peered at me for a long while before shuffling inside and settling in the chair on the right with a hefty groan.

"Don't dawdle, Yarleer," she said in a crochety voice. "You either, Kreelevar. I wish to return to my residence and make a pot of tea. My back veranda and a more comfortable chair await me."

Should I purchase cushions for her next visit? Another odd thought. I'd never considered her backside and comfort thereof. Cora would shake her finger at me if she knew this was the first time it was occurring to me.

Irritated that I was second-guessing my actions based on what she'd think of them, I stomped inside, slamming the door while the elders sat on the chairs.

The surprise on Yarleer's lined face had fled, replaced with his usual sneer. With him, I walked on a tiny vine across a great cavern. I suspected only Moonsten's more moderate influence had kept Yarleer from asking me to leave the colony already.

I dropped down into my chair, noting it *was* hard. A few cushions wouldn't suggest I was softening. My comfort mattered and seeing to it would not make my orc leaders frown.

"We've been watching you," Yarleer stated.

I nodded, unsure what to say to that, since his statement could have many meanings.

"The village is not yet a cohesive unit," he continued. "We will not have this. *I* will not have this!"

Moonsten placed a restraining hand on his wrinkly arm jutting out from his long, flowing robe. "Now, now. Allow me to speak?" Her sparkling eyes met mine. "One would think you two were related."

This was not possible. He was no mighty orc.

Rather than rise and storm about the room as was

my usual behavior to Yarleer's sneers, I opted to listen. Perhaps I was growing older and relaxing.

Perhaps I listened to Cora more than I realized.

I stiffened my spine and shot them both a glare for good measure. "How do you expect me to make the village more cohesive?"

"That is your job, not ours, is it not?" Yarleer growled. "You lead, we follow."

Moonsten coughed. "To some extent. You understand his meaning, however."

I did, but how did he expect me to turn the bits and pieces of them into a unified group?

"Our buildings have been constructed," Moonsten said. "Stores are open, colonists have settled into their dwellings, but the people themselves have no structure. There is nothing being done to keep everyone happy."

My thigh muscles twitched. This conversation was heading in a direction I couldn't control. "They have what they need. *That* should make them happy."

Yarleer growled again. "This is why you will fail. Rest assured, we will not fail along with you."

My guts clenched. While I'd gotten this job through the Interplanetary Council, the elders had the final say on whether I would be allowed to remain beyond the six lunar cycle trial period. "The buildings are completed." I'd ensured that before starting my own.

Moonsten nodded, her sharp gaze pinning me in place.

"The shelves at the stores are full," I added. "The

baker's shelves as well. Everyone has plenty of food to eat."

Yarleer sneered. "Anyone could've seen to this. What we need is someone to make this a true village." His sniff rang out. "I believe you lack this ability."

A shocking thought occurred to me.

I had no idea how to make others happy. For that matter, I wasn't sure I knew how to make myself happy.

Only since Cora arrived had I smiled.

"You live up on your hill," Moonsten said, though her tone remained soft and kind. "Down here, we shuffle forward. We need something to shuffle toward. Do you understand?"

I didn't. Food. Water. Housing. What else was there?

I could feel the fragile world I'd struggled to build falling apart around me.

"Our town is an empty shell," Moonsten said. "We need someone to fill us to overflowing. A true leader can do this easily."

Happiness would do it, they said.

How in the world was I going to bring the village that?

# 36
## CORA

While Kreel hurried to his meeting, I crossed the street and sat on a bench in the lovely village square.

Flowers swayed in the breeze, releasing their heady scent. On the flat, grassy area between me and the fountain, three children played a game I'd never seen before. It looked like a lot of fun. I watched for a while to pick up the rules. The game looked easier to play with four arms, but I could understand the logistics.

I'd started to rise to join them when Kreel stomped up behind me. Funny how I could tell by his huffing and his feet slamming on the ground that it was him.

"Smile," he barked from behind me. He waved his hands to the stunned children who'd stopped playing to gape at him. "Smile, I said!"

The lower lip of one of the kids quivered.

I leapt up, raced around the bench, and grabbed

Kreel's hand, tugging him over to the kids who looked up at him in near horror.

Sitting, I dragged him down beside me.

"This is your ball." I held up a round ball, the biggest of the three, though it was barely larger than my thumbnail.

"I have enough balls," he said with a touch of humor.

And that was why it was so easy to be with him. He might grouch a lot, but he was a softie inside. He just needed to be shown it was okay to let his inner marshmallow shine through.

"The point of the game is to tap your ball into the other balls, knocking them into the circle."

"I don't understand," he said, his brow tight.

"Watch and I'll show you."

Taking a tiny mallet from one of the children, I carefully tapped the larger ball into the small ones. One of the kids squealed as the ball smacked into the others, sending them flying well beyond the circle.

The little girl giggled. She smiled at me, but her expression froze when it passed onto Kreel.

"You do it next," I said, crawling over to retrieve the big ball and dropping it into Kreel's hand—that I had to lift and open. "Do it. I promise, you'll enjoy this."

His eyes sparkled, but I could tell he was still confused. "If you promise, I believe you."

Aw. This was another reason I liked him. He held no doubts about me.

The twin boys stared at Kreel with eyes wider than a

fawn standing in a road with a fleet of shuttle cars bearing down upon it.

Kreel frowned at the ball resting in his hand. "I don't—"

"You can do eet," the little girl said. She climbed into his lap and stared up at him. Her thick strands of pink hair lifted in the breeze, and I'd never seen anything cuter than her sitting there while Kreel's hands fluttered around her. I could tell he wasn't sure if he should support her, so she didn't fall from his lap, or nudge her away.

My heart just about stopped. She was so tiny compared to him. Everyone was, actually, though the top of the adult Ulorn's heads came nearly to Kreel's shoulders.

She must've sensed he was someone who could be trusted, and she was spot-on with that.

He swallowed. "Would you . . ." He pinched his eyelids shut. "Would you show me, yarling?"

Now *I* wanted to crawl into his lap. Kiss him. Maybe he wasn't the type of guy who wanted to come out of his shell and interact much with the world around him, but I sensed he hid his loneliness. No one would come near him as long as he snapped whenever they were around.

The little girl climbed off his lap. She took his hand still holding the ball and guided it to the ground. Kreel rose to his hands and knees and watched her intently.

I spied movement on the other side of the park. A female Ulorn hurried this way, her hands clutched against her mouth. Two other females rushed behind her, looking equally horrified.

Did they think Kreel would hurt their children?

One stopped when she was a few feet away, but rather than snatch up her child as I suspected she longed to do, she dropped down onto a bench. She watched, her hands gripping the bench seat tight enough that all four of her hands blanched.

My attention was drawn to someone eclipsed by the shadow of a building across the street. I stared that way but couldn't make out who it was. Was someone else watching us?

"Like dis," the little girl said, pulling my attention back to her and Kreel. She went around to the side of Kreel's arm and helped him position the ball. Handing him a tiny mallet, she sent him a fang-filled smile. The tiniest horns jutted up from her rich, pink hair. "And dis." She guided his hand to hit the ball.

It soared across the grass and clinked when it hit the others, sending two of them flying in the wrong direction but the third teetering toward the circle.

The little boys leaned forward, holding their breath.

The ball wavered into the circle and came to a stop.

"Yes," the little girl cried, leaping to her feet.

Kreel sat back on his butt and grinned. Pure happiness suffused his face.

The little girl leaped onto him, her four arms wrapping around his neck and head. "Did it!"

"I did it," Kreel gulped out. "I did."

# 37
## KREEL

"I need your help," I said as my wagon rumbled out of town. In the back, I'd loaded more bread, fruit, and vegetables and secured the oven so it wouldn't crush them.

Cora sat on the bench with me, leaning against my side.

I savored how warm her arm was around my back and the way she kept glancing up at me through her thick lashes. Orcs didn't have lashes, and that was a true crime. I wanted to stroke hers. Kiss them when she was asleep.

"Nah. Surely you don't need help," she said. I could tell she was teasing by the light in her eyes. "I thought you were in complete control of the entire world."

I huffed, recognizing she was right in this assessment. "I'm not always in control," I hedged.

"No!"

My grin slipped out. I couldn't stop it. So I directed it her way.

She leaned against me further, placing her hand on my thigh.

The gesture woke my cock, not that it went to sleep very often. But I sensed this was one of those moments she referred to where she wanted to touch, but not sex.

It felt nice to have her stroke me. It suggested affection. I could see how this would be enjoyable even if it did not lead to pounding into her.

Meanwhile, my hearts were in complete turmoil, both shouting I needed to do all I could to win her, that they'd host a coup if she left.

"How can I help you?" she asked.

"I'm at a loss," I said carefully. "I know how to build a village. How to encourage commerce. But I do not know how to turn these structures and the people living within them into a cohesive village."

"What kind of cohesion are you looking for?"

"I need to make them happy."

"I suspect all this comes from your meeting with the two older Ulorns?" she asked.

"You are correct. The elders told me I must bring happiness to the village." I pinched my eyelids shut but only for a tick. If I didn't pay attention to the culairs, they would bolt. They tested me always.

Much like the elders.

And Cora.

"Happiness?" she said. "That's easy."

I grumbled. "It is not easy. I have no idea how to make anyone happy."

"You make me happy," she said softly.

"That is sex. My copious cum makes you happy." I was only half-joking.

She blinked at me for a moment before her lips curled upward. "You are in love with your cum."

"All orcs are."

"But your cum isn't making me happy."

My jaw dropped, and I partly turned to gape at her. "Say this isn't so."

"Good one." She nudged my arm, her grin restored because I'd attempted humor. "It's lovely cum, and the actions leading up to its deposit are fun, but that's not what I meant when I said you make me happy."

Confusion filled me. "How else does an orc make his —" I almost spilled the word, *mate* again, though she might not have noticed. Shaking my head, I continued. "How does an orc make anyone happy?"

"You sound like a glum bunch."

"Humor is rare in an orc clan."

"Why?"

"Why not?" I wasn't sure where she was taking this. "Orcs work. We build. We ensure everyone in the clan has what they need—"

"What you're saying is completely admirable, but none of those things take care of someone's emotional needs." She held up her hand before I could speak. "Back up a second there. Those things do give emotional support to some extent. I mean, you can be emotionally satisfied if your belly is full of food and," she shot me a sly glance, "other parts are full of cum, especially if you have a solid roof overhead."

I grunted, pleased she'd acknowledged the might of my cum.

"But to truly make someone happy, you have to feed the full spectrum of their emotions."

"I have no idea how to do this." Even to my own jutting ears, I sounded worried. I couldn't tell her how desperately I hoped not to fail, how I didn't want to be sent back to my clan with shame hanging over my head.

How I wished to please not only the village, but her.

"You satisfied the little girl's emotional needs by playing a game with her."

"Then I will play this game with the elders. They will be happy, and I can then go back to working on my house."

"You can work on your house at the same time, but it's going to take more than a simple game to make everyone happy."

"Many games?" I suggested, though I could see what she meant.

"It needs to be something bigger."

"Like what?"

"Why don't we do something as a community?" she asked as I drew the wagon to a stop in front of my house.

I was grateful she was helping. Already, I'd learned something. Emotions were tied to happiness.

Cora had indicated my cum wasn't enough, and that

stung, but she wasn't an orc. She wouldn't be as enthused about gushing white stuff as me or a female of my species.

As for a community event, what did we have planned for the next week other than me driving my . . . hammer into her? I liked that term. It was clever, as was Cora for thinking of it.

But for the first time, I realized she might wish to share the company of someone other than me. A full lunar cycle was a long time to spend alone with an orc who was desperate to fuck her.

It was important I make Cora happy, not just the villagers.

If she was content, maybe, just maybe, she wouldn't want to leave me when my mating frenzy was finished.

The culairs shuffled their feet, and from the way their ears poked forward, they were eager to get back to their eggs. I needed to release them from their harnesses and lead them to their pen.

The female had laid ten, too many for a normal clutch, and she would race to them. Ten might be too many, but I hadn't been able to make myself destroy any.

This could mean I was already on the right path to learning the happiness lesson with Truffle and Poochie. I allowed them to decide how many eggs was enough.

"We could organize a huge game," I said. "And make all the community attend and play."

"I think we should do something adults enjoy instead. And we'll *ask*. We won't demand they attend."

I lifted my brows. "What do you suggest?"

"What would you think of organizing a potluck supper?"

# 38
## CORA

"What is this poot-luke sooper?" Kreel asked. He climbed off the wagon and turned, lifting me off to plunk me on the ground beside him.

"Everyone brings a dish, and we share the meal. They'll eat whatever we bring, and we'll do the same."

"What if I don't like what they serve?" he said. "I eat meat. Only meat. You heard Breelair a week ago. They don't have meat."

"She said it was too difficult to come by." A spark of an idea hit me. "What if you hunted and brought enough meat for the entire village? That would make them happy."

"How are emotions connected with meat?"

My mind was so dirty. So was my mouth. And my hand. I advanced on him and stroked his cock through his pants. "This meat makes me happy."

He frowned down at me. "You wish for sex? I thought we were discussing meat?"

"It's a joke. Meat stick. Meat nugget. Hunk of meat." I tilted my head, but I could see he wasn't getting it. "Anyway, if you hunt, you can bring big steaks to the potluck supper. That'll impress them. I'll make cookies since this community is sorely lacking in sweets."

"I'm still not sure how food brings about emotional happiness." He nudged me backward, holding my arms so I wouldn't fall.

I wasn't sure where we were going, but I was along for the ride.

"If people are having fun, laughing and enjoying good food, it brings emotional satisfaction." I said. "If they're doing it together, it builds unity. This is one of the ways you can please the elders."

"I like this idea," he said slowly. "I will tell them they must appear at this poot-luke sooper tomorrow."

My back nudged against the table. Kreel bent forward and started nibbling at my neck with his tusks. They were big, mighty things, but somehow, he could be gentle with them.

Heat swirled through me, and my limbs limped out. I wanted to focus on the conversation.

"Let's give them some advance notice," I said as he undid his pants.

A hint of a smile curled his lips. "Will five days from now be enough?"

"It should be. We invite them." I stressed invite. "We want them to attend willingly."

"I am all about willing." His cock sprang free from the front of his pants, erect and ruddy with need. He started bunching my skirt up in his fingers and leaning me backward.

I hopped up onto the table and inched my butt close to the edge. My mouth had gone dry, and I'd completely forgotten what we were talking about.

His tail coiled around my right ankle, tugging it wide. The gesture was repeated with my left leg.

He stooped down and licked me between the legs, gliding his tongue inside me. His fingers stroked my clit, and I was soon a panting wreck.

Rising over me, he centered his cock at my core. His gaze met mine, hooded and filled with incredible need. The feeling was matched within me.

"What were we talking about?" I asked, all breathy.

"My meat stick," he growled as he drove himself inside me. "You were longing for my anaconda meat stick."

# 39
## KREEL

I rode her hard while she whimpered and moaned beneath me. My strokes kept driving her across the table, but it was fun tugging her back, seating her on my shaft once more.

When she gasped and shuddered beneath me, I shot my cock inside her to the hilt and gave way to my own orgasm.

My cum filled her as always, and what could be better than that?

I bent over her after, kissing her gently. "Happy now?"

She hummed, her palms rubbing my shoulders. "Very."

"See? This was all you needed."

"You're right," she said, and I swore I heard laughter in her voice, though when I lifted my head, I didn't see it on her face. "All I need in life is your cum to make me happy."

I grumbled, sure there was a tease hidden in her words, but unable to find it. She smiled, but it was soft, not mocking.

After we'd straightened our clothing, I snapped my finger. A rilleen flew out of the forest and landed on the table.

"A bird," Cora said. "A big bird just . . . landed nearby. Don't kill it."

I chuckled. "I have no intention of killing it. It was too difficult to catch and train."

"What did you train it to do?"

I scrawled a note to the elders and secured it to the rilleen's leg.

"It's a carrier pigeon?"

"I do not believe so," I said.

"Long ago on Earth, they used birds to carry messages."

I lifted the rilleen. "Take this to Moonsten." The bird took off, soaring toward town.

"Just like that?" Cora asked. "That's some training."

I tapped her nose, a gesture that showed affection without giving too much away. When she tried to nip at it, I grinned. "I am the best trainer, don't you agree?"

Her eyebrows lifted. "I guess it depends on what you mean by training."

"You are correct." I strode toward the house. "Time to get to work."

"Work, work, work. I'm glad you sent the message. Will they send a reply?"

"Yes. They will agree."

"I'm glad you're confident about this," she said as she followed me to where we had to apply trim around the siding panels. Once we placed the windows, we would add trim there too.

"Of course I am confident," I said in all seriousness. "I commanded them to attend."

She stared at me, stunned. "Please tell me you didn't make demands."

I laughed, and she looked even more stunned than before. "I politely invited them, but I believe they will agree."

"You surprise me, Kreel."

Sometimes, I surprised myself.

"I guess you're seeing how doing things can make them happy," she said.

"I can see this," I said. "You give me sex, which is doing something for me, and it makes me very happy." My hearts beat only for her, speeding around in my chest whenever she was around.

As we worked on the house, her words and council sunk further into my mind.

"Growing up, I believed having things was what made a person happy," I said as I secured the final bit of trim. We could haul the windows out of my shed tomorrow.

"If you have nothing," she said. "Even the clothing on your back can give you a feeling of joy."

Since there was light left in the sky, I urged her inside. We could start working on my kitchen. It would be nice to cook my meat inside, especially when it was raining.

"As I told you before, I never knew my father," she spontaneously said as she helped me secure an interior panel. It was covered with a smooth, pale surface that would look nice in my kitchen.

Funny how I was taking happiness in seeing how something appeared. Another emotional need being satisfied?

"Why did you never know him?" I asked, expecting her to tell me he had been a distant person or busy with business.

"My mom never told me who he was."

"Orcs don't do this," I said.

"Then you're lucky. You may not remember your parents, but at least you have names for them." She didn't sound bitter, more resigned.

"I wish sometimes I did remember them. Maybe they would've been nicer to me than the male who raised me."

She gulped. "Was he mean?"

Pausing in the center of the room, I determined I'd place all the walls first. Once they were painted, and the ceiling, too, I could install cabinets. I'd planned a sink, something only the wealthiest orcs had within their homes. Most washed their dishes, though they kept few, in sinks outside with drawn water.

"Indifferent, I guess you could call our leader," I said.

"Why raise kids if you don't like them?"

"He was in charge of everything. It was his role. But we are not discussing me. We are talking about you."

"We don't need to do this."

"I want to know," I growled out. I wouldn't force her to speak, but I wanted to understand Cora and that included how she'd grown up. "You had a mother," I prompted.

"More or less. She mostly left me to raise myself. We don't get along."

"Then you are as alone as me." My hearts hurt for her. It was a different feeling than the one I got when we had sex. Then, my hearts surged upward as if they could fly all the way to the moons. Now, they had sunk as if burrowing into the ground.

"I guess we are," she said softly. Looking down, she blinked fast.

"I am sorry."

"I thought you didn't like that word." She secured the panel and strode over to the pile in the room adjoining this one.

When she hurt, so did I, a new experience for me. "I hardened myself while growing up. I don't like pain."

"Few do."

Taking her arm, I tugged her closer. She smelled good. A touch of sweat from her exertion. A hint of the sex we'd shared. And a generous dose of fresh air. Pure Cora. "Maintaining a tough exterior isn't always a good thing." Only now did I see this. "This wall I built around myself keeps others out."

"This is profound, Kreel." She studied my face, but I

was so stoic, she saw nothing. I never gave anyone a weapon to use against me.

This was wrong, at least with Cora. She wouldn't use my emotions to hurt me. I knew this in my hearts.

Drawing in a breath became a challenge. Growing up, if I felt this way, I would run from the others and hide. This was how I'd found my mine, diving into a hole in the ground when others chased me.

I didn't want to hide from Cora.

I tightened my arms around her.

She resisted, but only for a moment before leaning close, breathing against my skin.

"You want sex," she said dully.

"I always want sex, but for now, I just want to hold you."

Her body quivered. "Is your mating frenzy waning?"

"It is not that." I suspected with her; my frenzy would never wane. Yes, the overwhelming urge to fuck would fade, but I'd always want to be with Cora.

It wasn't all about filling her with my cum, though that was a delightful thing to do. I wanted to see her smile even when I didn't fuck her.

I needed to make her truly happy, but how?

"You're not a hugger," she said. "But I like it."

What could I do that she would love? Because I wanted her to love me.

This. I could do this.

I huffed. "I am a hugger now."

# 40
## CORA

"I will put on a shirt, and we will go to town to collect your clothing," Kreel said two mornings later.

We'd spent the last few days placing the windows and securing trim around them. Then, we'd continued hanging the kitchen walls. After eating each day, we went to bed.

The all-night-long sex was amazing—*Kreel* was amazing.

And strangely enough, he held me all through the night, kissing the top of my head when I'd almost fallen asleep. My eyelashes when he thought I was asleep.

His warmth and sweetness were worming into my soul.

"Why wear a shirt?" I asked. "You never have before."

He paused. "I wish to appear . . . appropriate. Respectful."

"Shirtless is disrespectful?"

"I never thought so before, but I do now."

"Okay." Personally, I loved his shirtless look, but I could see what he meant. He wanted to be taken seriously by the villagers. Wearing a shirt into town might be the first step in that direction.

"I'm all set," I said, brushing the construction dust off my dress that I'd washed out each evening. "I'll be glad to have more clothing."

"Do not forget these," he said. He rushed to the trees. I frowned, taking in the tiny clothesline he'd strung. He returned and handed me my panties.

I blinked at them. "They're not clean. I forgot to wash them last night." He'd made me forget, and I didn't regret it for one second.

"*I* washed them."

Some women would squirm at the thought. "You did?"

"They are yours."

"They're only around because you haven't clawed them to shreds yet."

"I will not," he vowed.

"I don't understand."

"I know what it is like to have nothing. These are yours." He waved to my sole pair of underwear. "I will cherish them because they belong to you."

He got it. He got me. When I stared at my ratty pair of underpants, I nearly cried. "Thank you."

"It is wrong of me to shred everything you wear," he said softly. "We will buy all the clothing they have at the store that fits, plus order more from other planets, but I will no longer rip them."

It was hella sexy when he did it, but it also wasn't easy working on a construction site while wearing a dress.

"Just rip some of them," I said as a compromise. "Leave others alone." Like my dress that was sadly worn from wearing it all the time. I still loved it. When I left, I'd take it with me. Then I could pull it out sometimes and touch it and remember this month with Kreel.

His head tilted, and he studied my face. "We will discuss the shredding of your clothing after you have a suitable quantity."

He was quiet today, but I didn't mind. We'd shared some heavy conversation over the days before, and he could still be contemplating what I'd said.

I'd strive to keep things light as we headed into town.

Before we harnessed the culairs, I entered the pen and walked over to admire the eggs. Each was as red as the culairs scaled skin. About a foot in length, they nestled within the soft mound of dried grass. "What are you going to do with all the babies?"

"Me? They are Truffle and Poochie's babies, not mine."

"Some people would sell them."

"The villagers are wary of culairs. They would not buy them from me."

"I didn't see any in town," I said. "I thought they kept them behind the buildings or something."

"They prefer simple beasts of burden." He flashed a tusk-filled smile that melted my bones. "I prefer those that are wild."

It was all I could do not to leap on him. Somehow, with a simple gesture and a few words, he could make me crave him.

He tapped my nose. "Come now. None of that. I will fill you full of my cum later." He waited near the wagon to lift me up onto the bench.

"I'm already full of cum." It was a good thing he had a lot of towels. I'd cut up a bunch and washed them out with my undies each evening.

"As you should be," he said smugly, gaining his seat on the bench with one bound. He shifted the reins, and the culairs placidly strode down the hill toward town.

His appetite for my body hadn't slowed, but we still had about a week before his mating frenzy would wane.

As for the awakening, I'd quizzed him a couple of times, but he still hadn't given me a straight answer. It must be the trigger for his frenzy.

"I understand why you wouldn't want to sell Truffle and Poochie's children, but they'll have more eggs, right?" He nodded. "Which means they'll overrun the place. Unless you plan to release them into the forest."

"I had not thought of this. I could ask them what they wish me to do with their yarlings."

He must be joking, but I remembered the bird he'd trained to carry messages. Perhaps he could communicate with the culairs. He'd figured out how to communicate with me.

"Occasionally, those from other planets reach out, seeking culair pups. If Truffle and Poochie agree, I could gift the pups to others who promised to treat them well."

"Are you allowed to send a species from one planet to another?"

"On occasion, and with the permission of the Interplanetary Council."

"If you did that and asked Truffle and Poochie to lay less eggs, you could keep the population from overrunning the planet."

"This is a good idea."

My pulse surged. I was silly to be so into his praise, but he gave it sparingly.

"Will these fade?" I asked, tracing my finger along one of his tattoos.

"What do you mean?"

I really hated naming it. In a week, we'd hold the potluck. It was ironic that it would take place the day before I'd have to leave.

"These markings. Do they go away once your frenzy ends?"

"No," he barked. He glared at the road; his jaw tight.

I'd done something to irritate him, though I wasn't sure what it could be.

"They look good," I said as a peace offering.

"They do."

It was going to hurt to board a shuttle. No, it was going to hurt to leave Kreel. Falling in love with him had been an unwise move on my part, but I couldn't help myself. He made me laugh. He made me swoon. He'd wormed his way into my heart and there was no throwing him out.

Hell, I was even going to miss his cum, though I'd never tell him. His ego was big enough already.

Actually, that wasn't true. He didn't have much ego; he used bravado and a gruff manner to protect himself from hurt. I hadn't seen it right away, but I did now.

He was an orc.

I was a human. Two vastly different species.

But maybe we were more alike than I'd realized.

# 41
## KREEL

As we drove into town, a few villagers called out greetings. They even displayed smiles. At first, I thought their welcome was for Cora, but then the shoemaker, Vivund, held up his hand.

I brought the culairs to a stop beside him.

"Wonderful idea about the poot-luke sooper, Kreel-evar Nohmal Trirag Grikohr," he said, surprising me that he remembered my full name.

"Kreel," I said. "Please call me Kreel."

"Of course." He nodded to Cora. "Will you be bringing a dish to the event?"

"I will, a dessert," she said with a smile.

"What is a dee-cert?"

"Believe me, you are going to be astounded."

Vivund frowned. "Only edible items are to be offered."

She snickered. "You'll be able to eat them."

"Them?" he gulped.

"They're not alive."

His hands fluttered at his neck. "You will kill them first."

She burst into laughter. "They will never be alive."

"Ah, I see." His frown deepened. "I really . . . must go. I do look forward to the poot-luke, however. Goodbye!" Whirling, he fled across the street, shooting terrified glances at us over his shoulder.

"Something went wrong with that conversation," Cora said.

"I imagine word of your crew-kees will spread through town quickly." I clicked the reins, directing the culairs to the store. "Some will be excited. Others . . ."

"Will act like him. They're good. Yum, actually. I promise."

"Then I cannot wait to taste them." I not only said it, but I also meant it.

"There you are," Breelair said, half-dancing from the store as I hitched the wagon. "How are you?"

I waited for Cora to speak. The two females were friends. Me and Breelair? I imagined she'd run as fast as Vivund had if I started chatting.

Leaning forward, Breelair tapped my shin. "Are you awake, Kreelevar?"

Cora's laugh rang out. "He's tired." She leaned against me. "Poor baby was up all night."

I was only up some of the time. My cock was not always erect.

"You speak to me," I said, staring in amazement at Breelair.

"I do, Kreelevar. I asked how you are."

"Kreel. Call me Kreel."

Cora poked my side, though gently.

"Please," I added.

Breelair blinked slowly. "I still cannot believe you want me to call you . . ." Her brow ridge rose even higher. "All right. *Kreel*."

"Thank you for asking. I am well." I thought about discussing cum but wasn't confident she would be thrilled to hear about my latest load. In an orc community? Definitely. Here? Lots of running away would be involved.

It surprised me that I cared about offending them. But when Cora smiled and hopped off the wagon, taking Breelair's arm to hurry with her back in the store, I understood.

She was right. Doing things for others and treating them kindly made a difference.

I followed them inside.

"Cora needs lots of clothing," I announced.

"You are kind to provide so well for your employee," Breelair said.

"I fired her."

Breelair's smile fell. "Oh." She shot a horrified look Cora's way. "Would you like a job here?"

"Oh, I'm just hanging out with Kreel now," Cora said.

"Hanging . . .?"

"We're kinda dating," Cora said, holding up another dress against the front of her body, this one in red.

Breelair clapped her four hands together. "Oh, like me and Aircorn!"

"Yup," Cora said.

The baker and Breelair . . . I shook my head, unable to picture the two of them together. Perhaps he also had lots of cum. That would explain his appeal.

The dress made Cora's hair shine and her skin glow.

I waved to Breelair.

She nodded and leaned over the counter, keeping her voice low. "I'll fix it quickly and add it to the rest."

"Thank you."

Color rose to her face as she bowed. "You are welcome . . . Kreel."

The change in everyone was amazing. I waited for it to end.

We stopped at the baker's and bought more bread.

Aircorn glowered, which was almost reassuring. I glowered back as orcs do.

After gathering our possessions—plus extra loaves of bread and crocks of butter—we left town.

As I drove the beasts down the main thoroughfare, Moonsten called out from the wooden walkway.

I stopped the wagon, but before she could start across the street in her painfully slow shuffle, I jumped off the wagon and went to her.

"Yes?" I asked, striving to keep my demeanor polite. It was hard not to snap at everyone, but I suddenly had a wish to make them happy. Perhaps it was my waning frenzy.

Or perhaps I was changing. For better or worse, and solely due to Cora.

"This poot-luke," she said.

I tightened my spine, waiting for her to say we must not do it.

She tapped my arm with her stick. "I like this idea." Her rheumy gaze drifted to Cora. "I believe you had help with this plan."

"She's amazing," I said, then realized I was gushing. "Isn't she?" My words squeaked out, much to my dismay.

I was a wreck, but I couldn't host the irritation to snap and snarl about it.

"Do not let her go," Moonsten said.

"Staying needs to be her decision." I might talk her into things, but I refused to push for something like that.

Moonsten bobbed her head. "You have gotten wiser, my son. Yarleer will be pleased."

I scratched the back of my neck. "I'm not sure anything could please Yarleer."

"Do not give up hope. He will one day like you."

I wasn't sure I hoped for that, actually. My real wish was that he'd avoid me forever.

"This poot-luke will bring us together, and then we will send our final report to the Interplanetary Council."

"Report?"

Her sharp gaze met mine. "You didn't know your ongoing position here was pending our final approval?"

I did, but I thought the Council would somehow decide on their own. The elders had the final say?

She cackled. "Your face needn't be so solemn. You are doing well, Kreelevar. Very well."

---

It was the final night of my frenzy and the evening of the poot-luke sooper. We took the wagon to town as the sun started to slink toward the horizon. In the back, I'd carefully placed the bowls with large cuts of meat I'd seared to perfection over the fire.

Cora had deferred helping me work on the house all afternoon, stating she had to prepare her own offering. Odd smells drifted my way as she worked, but she refused to let me taste a sample, stating I'd have to wait until after the meal like everyone else.

I hoped they weren't disappointed with our offerings and not because I needed their approval to stay.

I *wanted* to stay.

Even more, I wanted Cora to remain here with me as my forever mate. I hadn't asked. I was waiting for her to state that this was her wish, as all orc females do.

When we reached the village, I directed the culairs to the edge of town where I'd helped the villagers construct a huge barn. I thought they'd use the barn to raise culairs, but they stated they intended to use the building for a market at the end of each week.

Music and loud voices greeted us.

"This is it," Cora said. Quivering, she hugged her arms. "I hope this goes well."

"I have tried, and that is all I can do," I said. This

meal was important, but the change I'd seen in the village since Cora arrived made me happy.

An interesting realization. I was happy, and it wasn't only because Cora was by my side.

I'd found a place I could call home.

# 42

## CORA

I bit my lower lip as I carried my platter of cookies inside. I'd made pretty much a billion sugar cookies this afternoon, the first ones burning, the second batch tasting like sawdust. Eventually, I'd gotten the recipe to work with my limited ingredients, and the last batch came out perfect.

With a grunt, Kreel hefted his tubs full of meat, placing one on each shoulder.

If my fingers were free, I'd cross them, hoping everything would go okay. Instead, I settled for crossing my toes, though that made it a challenge to walk.

I wanted the villagers to be happy with his potluck dinner offering.

Even more, I wanted Kreel to feel as if he fit in.

"There you are," someone cried as we stood in the doorway. My tension started to ease as many called to me and Kreel.

Even Vivund inched closer, though his gaze remained

locked on my cookies as if he thought they'd leap off the platter and attack him.

"Can I help with that?" Vivund asked Kreel. "I could bring one of the tubs to the table."

When Kreel handed one over, Vivund staggered. Another male rushed to him, and each took a side. They carried it to the table, exclaiming when they spied the mounds of meat inside.

Breelair hurried over and took the platter from me. "So many exciting dishes. I imagine yours will fit in nicely. This is such a wonderful idea."

Kreel rocked on his heels and beamed.

I linked my arm through his and hugged his side, smiling up at him. "You're amazing, Kreel."

He tugged me into his arms, giving me a big hug. "No, you are, Cora."

"Come along," Breelair said after she placed the platter of cookies on the table and rushed back to stand in front of us. "You'll sit with me and Aircorn?" She grinned. "We are hanging out tonight. Dating."

"We'd love to hang out with you two." I took Kreel's hand and tugged him over to the table. Aircorn glowered, but Kreel gave it back tenfold.

Aircorn's shoulders curled forward, but his spine loosened when Breelair dropped into the seat beside him.

Around us, everyone chattered. It didn't take long for Kreel and Aircorn to lighten up toward each other. They were soon talking about culairs and trees and—ugh—cum.

Breelair and I just rolled our eyes at each other.

"Excuse me," Moonsten called out. She rose and gave the entire gathering a smile. "I want to thank all of you for coming tonight and especially Kreelevar for organizing the event."

Cheers erupted from the crowd.

"I am proud of the community we are building here, and we have Kreelevar to thank for ensuring we had safe, snug homes, this barn for the market and this event, and our delightful village. We are secure here for the first time in our lives. We no longer need to hide from invaders."

"Never," Kreel vowed, pressing his fist to his chest. "I will protect you all."

"Exactly," Moonsten said, bobbing her head.

Even Yarleer no longer glowered. His neutral gaze drifted over Kreel, and it wasn't a smile, but it could be the start of acceptance.

"Let us dine," Moonsten cried.

Everyone got up and shuffled over to the buffet table. I marveled at what Kreel had put together. Sure, he'd gone to town a few times alone to help coordinate this, but he'd pulled off something special.

We ate, and exclamations rang out about the meat Kreel had provided.

"I will hunt often and deliver it to town," he said, his face shining with pride.

The villagers consumed everything except my cookies, which none touched.

Breelair was the only brave soul to take one from the platter. It sat in front of her.

Aircorn frowned at it and whenever she reached out to lift it, he nudged her side.

"They're good," I said limply. I'd taken three.

Kreel grabbed one of mine and stuffed the entire thing into his mouth. As he chewed, his face changed from reservation to bliss.

"These are . . . amazing! Crew-kees are the most wonderful thing in the world next to Cora!"

As if the floodgates opened, the villagers rose and rushed to the platter.

Soon, everyone had taken one, and I was grateful I'd made enough. Munching and groans of pleasure rang out as the cookies were consumed.

"Make more," someone yelled.

"For the next poot-luke sooper!"

Kreel put his arm around my shoulders and squeezed. I sat back in his embrace, and my smile couldn't get bigger.

I was going to miss these people. This place.

And Kreel.

# 43
## KREEL

After friendly conversation that felt awkward to me because it served no obvious purpose, everyone rose and pushed the tables near the walls. Someone backed into a corner and started playing a stringed instrument, singing along with it. Villagers danced in the open space, leaping around with their four arms flailing.

"Whoa," Cora said, her jaw quivering and her eyes wide as she watched them. "I've never seen anything like this before."

"You haven't danced?" I asked. Even orcs enjoyed moving like this to music.

"Have you?"

"I believe for you, tiny human, tonight is the time to try dance." I lifted her off her feet and twirled her through the room, bumping into my villager friends. My nervousness disappeared, and I started tipping my head back and bellowing at the ceiling. Soon, everyone was doing the same thing, banging into each other and laughing between shrieks.

Cora clung to my shoulders, her feet dangling in the air, and there was nothing better than the feel of her in my arms. Her deep laughter rang out.

I hated knowing she'd soon leave me. How could I ask her to stay? She had a life before she met me, and it waited for her to return. I'd thought I'd have time to talk her into remaining, but what could I offer? I still didn't know if the village would accept me as a long-term manager. They might ask me to leave.

Cora would not fare well in orc society.

I had a place with my clan, but no true home. My credits could buy something, but would Cora welcome trailing behind me until I found a decent place to settle?

My life was too uncertain. Begging her to be a part of it would be wrong.

My hearts were going to ache for her forever.

I stopped whirling and leaned against the wall to catch my breath, though I didn't put Cora down.

She looped her arms around my neck, seemingly content to remain close. We had tonight. I would love her the best I could to show her what she meant to me. If I did it right, if I convinced her what we had was amazing, she might ask to stay.

I growled, hating the uncertainty churning inside me.

"Is everything okay?" she asked with shadows lurking in her eyes.

Maybe I would ask her to remain by my side, and she

would say no. She could be tired of me. Tired of me filling her with cum. Orc behavior, I understood. Humans? She and her species remained a mystery.

Moonsten sidled over to us with Yarleer lurking behind.

"You have done well," she pronounced. "I have sent the missive to the Interstellar Council. If you wish to remain here with us, we will extend your contract for an indefinite time."

Cora smiled, but why did I sense her unease?

"What do you say?" Yarleer growled. "I assume thanks."

Normally, I'd snap at him, snarl and maybe stomp my feet to show him I was a mighty orc, and he was a puny Ulorn.

Lately, I'd held myself back because I wanted to look kinder in Cora's eyes.

Now, I only smiled. My grin might hint at the snarky feeling lurking inside me, but I no longer wished to behave in this manner.

"I say that I would like to stay," I said.

Yarleer huffed, but his face softened. I doubted he'd ever enjoy being in my company, but I hoped one day, we could start being friends. I didn't need his offer of friendship, but to continue helping this community, I needed to get along with everyone within it.

"Wonderful," Moonsten said, swaying to the music. Her long blue robe fluttered around her ankles. It had pockets and items bulged within them. Had she stuffed the last of the crew-kees inside? "I will notify the village, and we will plan another gathering to celebrate, perhaps in half a lunar cycle."

"That isn't necessary," I said, stunned that anyone would want to celebrate me remaining near them. In the past, most ran in the opposite direction. Orcs never minded, but we were a grumbly lot and snarling was an art form among them.

Cora remained silent, and she was definitely frowning.

When her breath caught, I turned to look in the direction she stared.

Six beings unlike any I'd seen before stomped into the room. One lifted his weapon and shot it toward the ceiling.

The music came to a screeching halt, and everyone backed away from the creatures.

"What is the meaning of this?" Moonsten cried.

I lowered Cora to her feet and nudged her behind me. With my fists clenched at my sides, I stormed toward them.

I came to a shuddering halt when one of them spoke.

"Cora, Cora, Cora," he drawled, his weapon pointed directly at her. "Come with usss, and we will leave everyone alone. Refuse, and we will take them allsss to the auctions."

# 44
## CORA

My past had caught up to me.

Kreel turned toward me, frowning. "What do they speak of? Do you know these creatures?"

I cringed but stepped forward to join him. "They're Vessars, the lizard mafia. They followed me from Earth."

"She owessss us moneyssss," the leader said.

"I don't." I lifted my chin. I didn't dare look at Kreel. How horrifying. I never should've come here. I'd endangered the people I was starting to care about.

I'd endangered Kreel.

I couldn't survive if something happened to him, because . . . because I loved him. When had that happened?

Shaking my head, I glared at the leader of the Vessars. "I don't owe you anything. You know that."

"Your cousin doessss."

"Go after him," I barked.

"Disappeared."

Something I should've done.

Kreel took my hand and squeezed it. "You can't have Cora, and you're not touching any of us."

Moonsten came up to stand on my other side. I tried to nudge her behind me, to protect her, but she shook her head, her hand straying to her pocket.

The other villagers backed up against the walls, leaving me, Moonsten, Kreel, and Yarleer in the center alone.

"Leave," Kreel growled, stomping toward them.

The Vessars tightened their grips on their weapons.

I snagged Kreel's arm, holding him back. "Don't. I'll go with them. Please."

"Yesss," the leader hissed. "Comesss wit us. We sell for high price. Pay cousinsss debt."

I pinched my eyes shut, but only for a second. I was more worried about my friends and Kreel being hurt than what would happen to me.

"She's not going with you," Kreel bellowed, leaping forward. He crashed into one of the Vessars, and they fell to the floor in a tangle of limbs.

The other Vessars rushed toward me.

I looked around for a weapon. Yes, a chair. I could break it and use one of the legs.

Moonsten stepped between us, pulling something from her pocket. Yarleer stood strong beside her.

Laser beams slammed into the ground in front of the Vessars, and they shrieked and came to a halt.

Moonsten grinned, holding a smoking gun in her hand. "Try again, lizard beasts. Next time, I will hit something you do not wish to lose." Her cackle rang out.

"Yes," Yarleer shouted. He pointed a gun toward the Vessars pinning Kreel to the ground. "Release him."

When they hesitated, Yarleer shot, hitting one in the back. With a groan, the Vessar tumbled off Kreel, falling to the floor with a solid thud.

The others rose and backed away, their hands lifting.

Yarleer nodded to Kreel. "Get up. Protect our Cora."

*Our* Cora?

"How much?" Kreel barked.

I rushed to him and helped him stand, though he didn't need assistance. My knees shook. I was the one who'd fall. "What are you doing?"

"How much is owed?" Kreel asked again.

The leader named a figure that made me gulp. My damn cousin. How could he take off after borrowing so much?

Kreel tapped on his wrist com, before tilting it toward them. "Enter your information, then get out of my town."

The leader did as Kreel asked.

After tossing me a slick smile, he turned and left, the others trailing him. The one Yarleer shot limped after them.

"I don't understand," I said, turning to face the crowd. Breelair came over and hugged me. Moonsten patted my shoulder.

Yarleer nodded, but his eyes no longer held irritation.

As for Kreel, he stood near the door, watching to

make sure the Vessars left. When he turned back our way, I lowered my head.

How could I face him?

"Why would we protect you, you ask?" Breelair said. "Because you are one of us. We are family. Kreelevar too."

Shame filled me, making my hands shake. I had to speak with him about this.

I walked over to him slowly, stopping in front of him. "Why did you pay them? It was too many credits."

"I couldn't do anything else," he said starkly, but I didn't know how to read his voice or his posture.

With the party over, everyone filed from the building, patting my arm and Kreel's as they passed.

Soon, we were the only ones left inside the building.

"We should go home," he said, turning toward the door.

Ah, yes. He had one more night of his frenzy left, and he'd want to get home for that.

It wasn't my home, though. Despite the kindness my friends had displayed, I had no place here to call my own.

As I followed him to the wagon, I tried to speak, but he held up his hand.

"No," he said.

I couldn't even drum up the anger to snap. It was over between us. The balloon had been popped, and there would be no fusing it back together again.

He helped me up onto the bench, but when he sat beside me, he made sure there was space between us.

Disgust at myself nearly overwhelmed me. He was

disappointed in me. He didn't want to look at me, touch me, or speak with me.

I said nothing as the culairs took us up the hill to his home.

After unhitching the beasts and putting them back into their pen, we walked toward my tent. Soon, he'd be able to stay inside his house. It would be finished, but I'd be long gone by then.

He stopped outside the tent. "My frenzy is over."

So, I wouldn't even have one last night with him before he sent me away.

A crater opened in my heart. He'd walk away, sleep someplace else tonight, and in the morning, a shuttle would be waiting. I could return to Earth without fearing the Vessars, but I didn't care about that.

All I could think of was how much I was going to miss Kreel.

"You're saying you don't need me anymore," I choked out, not looking up. I couldn't bear to see the disappointment on his face. I'd brought danger to this colony. He was responsible for keeping everyone safe. He walked on thin ice with the community already. I may have helped him secure his position, but I endangered it all over again.

I was surprised he didn't refuse to speak with me, surprised he didn't turn and stomp away.

"That's not true, Cora," he said softly.

I must've misheard him.

"It'll never be true," he said in a stronger voice. He

stroked his fingers along my jaw. "Would you look at me? Please?"

"You're saying please."

"I learned nice words like that one from a master."

I swallowed, but I still couldn't lift my face. I didn't want to see condemnation in his eyes.

"I need you for always, Cora," he said.

Wait a minute. I glanced up at him, taking in the stark craters on his beloved face. "What are you saying?"

His sigh huffed out.

My head tilted. "Tell me. If there's any time to be honest, to spell out your emotions, it's now."

"I love you," he grumbled.

My heart took flight, soaring into the night sky, but I remained grounded with Kreel, the orc of my dreams.

Of course, I couldn't resist teasing him. "You don't sound too sure of that, though you need to know I'm staying here with you. I'm not leaving. You'll have to pin me inside a shuttle to get me to go."

"You are mine." He swept me up and spun, his mouth seeking mine. "Love you. Love you. Love you." He punctuated each word with a kiss.

"I believe you," I said my arms and legs wrapped around him. There was no time better than this. No place I'd rather be than with this guy. "Do you want to know why?"

"I do," he said with a huff.

I grinned. "Because I love you too."

# 45

## EPILOGUE

### CORA

One Month Later

The culair eggs had hatched, and we'd spent most of our waking hours chasing them around.

"I need a better fence," Kreel said, lifting one of the pups up over the wooden structure that kept the adults inside. He dropped the bright red pup onto the ground, and it promptly scurried beneath the lowest pole.

Between finishing the inside of the house—which was almost done—and racing after the ten babies, we barely had time to be with each other.

At least the culair pups slept at night in their nest. This gave us a nice long stretch to snuggle in the big bed in the house's master bedroom. We did a whole lot more than snuggling, naturally.

One could say we did a lot of nailing. My Kreel did have a big hammer, and he loved using it. And I didn't even want to bring up how excited he was to keep delivering cum.

Wait until he found out. He'd be so proud, I'd never get him to shut up about it.

"My damn implant failed," I told him as he lowered two more of the pups back into the culair pen. He'd started adding a tight mesh of wire, but there were still a few spots left to cover. That would keep them contained until they'd left for their new homes.

He'd decided to give them all away, and the first person who'd begged for two would arrive today. Some alien trillionaire who owned his own planet. I expected a snooty guy. Gray hair. He'd look down his nose at us and sneer at the pups. My idea was a total cliché, but what did I know? I could be right.

"What do you mean, your implant failed?" Kreel asked, his brow wedging together.

"It failed." I flipped my arms up into the air. I wasn't that upset about this. We were mated and would remain together forever. What did a little implant failure mean when compared to that?

He shook his head and growled at the culair pup tiptoeing toward the opening in the fence. It slunk backward, snapping and snarling. Overall, they were tame, and they loved to cuddle. But whoever adopted that one was going to have their hands full until they'd showed it who was boss.

They were a complete mess, and I loved them.

Kreel froze. "Your implant has failed," he said slowly. He turned to face me, his eyes widening. "Your implant has failed!" Rushing to me, he scooped me up and spun me around. "My cum. My cum! It is amazing, is it not, mate?"

"It's about more than your cum," I said dryly, though my lips quivered. He was cute even when he was talking about spermies.

"You will have the first of our yarlings. The first!" He kissed me too fast for my taste. "We will have many yarlings. A full pack of them. At least ten like the culairs."

Ten? My brain solidified. Freakin' no way!

"Hold on there, buddy," I said, struggling to sound reasonable. "Slow down about the pack. We'll start with one, see how that goes, and then we can discuss more." I didn't mind the idea of a big family, but we'd just gotten together. I wasn't ready for more than that.

Although, it wasn't like I had much choice. Sure, there must be a way to renew my implant after our first yarling was born, but if this one had failed, what would keep others from doing the same?

"No more cum," I pronounced.

He pouted. "You enjoy it. It fills you and makes you slippery when I take you the second, third, and fourth times."

"I'm always slippery." He made me hot for him with just a simple look.

"I thought of something, and this time, I need to

insist. You will not work on the house any longer," he shouted.

"Of course I'll help you finish the house. I'm pregnant, not an egg that'll break if it hits the ground."

He scowled and stomped his feet. "You are in a delicate condition, and you must rest at all times."

"The more help I can give you, the quicker we'll get it finished. We're going to need bedrooms for the babies."

"Ah, you are right." His brow wedged deeply. "I will hire some of the villagers to help us finish."

I'd worried that I'd drained all his credits to pay off the Vessars, but he assured me he'd made more credits in his mine than we could spend in ten lifetimes. What he'd paid the Vessars hadn't even scraped the surface.

It appeared I was mated to an orc trillionaire.

I'd sold my property on Earth and sent a note to my mom. I doubted she flinched when she read my goodbye.

*So long,* I'd said. *Won't see you later. Don't write.*

My future—my world—was with Kreel.

"I don't mind the idea of hiring others to help, but I want to be a part of finishing our home," I said.

He lowered me to my feet but kept his arms around my shoulders. "You may hold the nails while I use my mighty hammer."

I was going to do a heck of a lot more than that, but it wasn't worth arguing about. He might fume and bellow, but he always saw things my way eventually.

I gave him a smile and was about to leap back into his arms and suggest we have some fun on the kitchen counter when someone cleared their throat nearby.

"Excuse me. I am Venge," he said, giving us curt nods. "I believe you are expecting me?"

I turned and leaned into Kreel's embrace.

Holy hotness, who was this guy?

While Kreel introduced us, I stared at the super-tall guy with blue scaled skin. He was slightly leaner than Kreel but still totally jacked if the fit of his tailored shirt and pants were anything to go by. He wore black boots, and he'd slung a jacket over his arm.

Oh, shit, this was the trillionaire, come to select two culair pups.

He squinted past us, taking in the pen and the woods behind it. Since my experience with wealthy guys suggested they behaved like complete assholes, I didn't expect anything else from him.

When Kreel mentioned Venge, I wasn't sure I wanted to give our precious pups to someone who might be mean to them or neglect them.

"They are beauties, aren't they?" he said softly. "Truly amazing."

His comment pleased me, but when he strode to the fence and stooped down onto his heels and extended his hand through the fence and to the pups, I was almost won over.

When he cooed and the pups sidled over to his hand and rubbed it, I decided he might be an okay guy after all.

"We haven't named them yet, but there are ten," I said, joining him at the fence.

Kreel leaned against the rail on my other side, his warm hand relaxed on the back of my waist.

"When I heard you were giving them away, I had to come immediately," he said, rising to stand with us. "I've admired this breed for ages. My life is lonely, and I hope . . ." His swallow went down hard. "I am eager to adopt two."

"We're only giving them to good homes," I said, stating one of the lines I'd practiced.

"I understand." Venge said. "What can I say to convince you that I will treat them kindly?"

"Tell me how you intend to take care of them."

"I have researched the breed, and I have already stocked their favorite foods."

"And training?" I asked.

"You have me there." He winced. "I will hire someone for that. My staff would be upset if they destroyed my home. I want them to be fully trained by the time they are grown."

"I know a good employment agency. Maybe get in touch with them for a culair whisperer?" If such a thing existed.

Kreel's bull in the China shop method of training worked, but kindness might make the entire process easier for Venge.

He took in me and Kreel standing close together, and I swore I read envy in his dark purple eyes.

"Do you have a mate to help you care for the pups?" Frankly, even one pup was a lot of work. I couldn't imagine anyone taking on two at the same time.

Although, Kreel and I somehow managed ten with the help of their parents.

"Sadly, I am not yet mated," he said. "Other than my staff, I live alone in a castle, which makes it a challenge to meet females." His gaze skimmed down my front, but I didn't sense anything icky in the gesture.

"Pick your pups, and you can go," Kreel barked. He'd softened a lot since I arrived, but his gruff orc manner still came through on occasion. "Two. No more."

I held back a chuckle. "If you want, you can climb inside the pen with them. Their parents, Truffle and Poochie, won't hurt you."

Venge frowned at the names, but a rumble in Kreel's chest kept him from asking any more questions.

He leaped over the fence rather than climbing, and once he hit the ground, the pups swarmed him. The size of small dogs and weighing less than five pounds, they rose on their back legs and planted the front ones on Venge's shins.

He stooped down and tugged them all close, falling back on his butt with a snort. His laughter rang out, and I hoped he found the mate he appeared to be seeking. He seemed like a nice guy.

After he selected the two who kept trying to escape, we placed them in carry pens for travel.

"What's the name of the employment agency?" Venge asked after the crates had been stacked inside his shuttle.

"The Intergalactic Employment Agency," I said. "I'm sure they'll be able to help."

"I will call them. And thank you." His gaze took in Kreel holding me close, and there was no mistaking his envy this time. "I wish you all the best with the other culair pups and what looks like your new home." His clawed hand swept toward it.

For one second, I swore his skin on his arm changed, as if it hardened into something resembling stone. Nah. I had to be imagining it. Something like that wasn't possible.

A shadow of pain flitted across Venge's face, and he tucked his arm behind his back.

Yeah, I wasn't going to ask what just happened. It wasn't any of my business.

"Thank you." With a dip of his head, Venge quickly left, climbing into his shuttle and closing the hatch. The ship took off, soaring toward the clouds.

"He'll be kind to them," I said.

"If he isn't, I will find him and smack him with my hammer," Kreel said. He leaned close and kissed me below my ear. "How about you mate? Would you like me to do some banging with my hammer?"

I spun in his arms and leaped on him. "I thought you'd never ask."

As he carried me toward our house and what I hoped was the kitchen counter, I grinned.

Who would've thought my grumpy orc boss would wind up being the guy of my dreams?

Now, if I could just get him to stop talking about cum.

I hope you enjoyed Kreel & Cora's story!
I had SO much fun writing this world.
If you'd like to meet their new youngling
Hrall in a Bonus Epilogue,
just sign up for my newsletter!

(If you already subscribe, I'll post a link there.)


If you'd like a peek at Leashing the Alien,
Venge & Jenny's romance, turn the page . . .


Venge is about to hire Jenny to tame his culair pups,
and Jenny will show Venge the love he's been missing.


If you'd like to read more of my books,
I have 2 boxed sets out – the complete series,
including bonus scenes!
Mail-Order Brides of Crakair
Brides of Driegon
They're also FREE to read in KU!

Have you checked out the shared world I wrote in,
called Shattered Galaxies?
Ravaged World is one of my favorites.
A tortured hero.
A woman stolen from Earth.
A dying world.

# ABOUT THE AUTHOR

Ava Ross is a *USA Today* Bestselling author of numerous titles. She fell for men with unusual features when she first watched Star Wars, where alien creatures have gone mainstream. She lives in New England with her husband (who is sadly not an alien, though he is still cute in his own way), her kids, and a few assorted pets.

# OTHER SERIES BY AVA

*Mail-Order Brides of Crakair*

*Brides of Driegon*

*Fated Mates of the Ferlaern Warriors*

*Fated Mates of the Xilan Warriors*

*Holiday with a Cu'zod Warrior*

*Alien Warrior Abandoned*
*(Shattered Galaxies)*

*Galaxy Games*

*Beastly Alien Boss*

You can find Ava's books on Amazon.

Sign up for Ava's Newsletter!

# LEASHING THE ALIEN

**I was hired to tame alien pets,
but my beastly alien boss is
determined to tame *me*.**

As a pet whisperer, I've yet to meet a snarling beast I can't turn into a purring pussycat. When a billionaire alien living in a castle on an isolated planet posts a job looking for someone to housebreak his pets, I'm confident I can train them to eat out of his hand instead of trying to bite his head off.

My growly boss has two rules. Don't touch him and remain inside my room at night. The first part's a challenge, because I have an overwhelming urge to nuzzle his neck and lick . . . his fingers. As for the second, I lie awake all night, struggling to ignore the howls echoing through the barren castle passages.

I might be here to train his pets to walk on a leash, but I'm beginning to suspect there's a beast in this castle who wants to train me.

*Leashing the Alien* is Book 2 in the Beastly Alien Boss Series. Each book is standalone and features a woman hired for an off-world job who meets a gruff alien who can't resist falling for his fated mate.

# CHAPTER 1
## JENNY

"Dearly beloved, we are gathered here today to bless Jennifer and Thurston Harold Willington the fifth's marriage . . ."

I tried to block out the reverend's words, but they sunk into my skin like battery acid. My cringing glance Thurston's way showed him grinning at me, horrifying lust in his eyes. The second the vows were spoken; he'd drag me to a bedroom and toss me on a bed. Or he'd throw me to the carpet in the hall outside the chapel and consummate this farce of a marriage.

Behind us, the guests watched raptly. My dad, who arranged this horrifying match between me and Thurston's family, kept his finger on his wrist com in warning. One wrong move on my part, and electricity would jolt through me. Not enough to knock me out, but enough to show me who was in charge of this situation.

Tears trickled down Mom's face, probably because

what's happening to me brought back memories of how her and Dad's relationship started.

Forced marriage was a family tradition, and no one had been able to escape its tight grasp.

Thankfully, my father agreed to my request for an outdoor wedding.

And the inclusion of a friend's pet doves.

The reverend beamed benignly at me and Thurston before scanning the gathered audience. "If there is anyone here who protests this union, speak now, or forever hold your peace."

On cue, the doves I'd worked with when my friend first got them flew down the aisle, aiming straight for me and Thurston. I was so grateful, I wanted to cry.

They saw me waiting. And they saw the finger gesture I made, a simple twirl that, to most, would mean nothing. To them, I was asking for the movements we'd practiced.

A pet whisperer, my friends laughingly called me, because I could turn even the most ferocious beast into a tail-wagging pup begging for kisses.

The doves soared up, then split and flew back toward where I waited. While most of the audience cooed in awe, assuming this was part of the service, others stared wide eyed. I held back my grin.

The birds dove toward my father.

He squawked, reeling back with his hands lifting. Titters and shrieks erupted from those gathered, but the birds had only one task in mind: to attack the person holding the controller. I'd practiced this with them for months after my engagement to Thurston was announced. First, I'd used a mannequin, then another friend who thought I was preparing a joke.

The crowd gaped, unsure if they should run or stay to watch the rest of the spectacle.

I kicked Thurston hard in the shin, and he grunted, releasing his hold on my wrist. I ripped away the band strapped to my ankle and flung it toward my father.

Pivoting, I leaped off the dais.

My mother smiled and nodded, and the birds flew toward my friend's house where she'd collect them and hide them from my father.

Thurston bellowed in outrage as I fled down the aisle. At the end, I darted through the archway ornately decorated with flowers, their cloying scent coating my nostrils.

Inside the tiny building attached to the back of the hotel where I prepared for this horrifying event, I grabbed the bag I'd hidden in the back of the closet. I didn't stop to change but wrenched open the outer door and raced into the main part of the hotel. I fled across the lobby and out onto the street.

Behind me, pandemonium reigned, but one shout rang out among them all.

"*Jennifer*," my father roared.

I didn't look back but ran down the street, big city buildings towering over me. My father owned three or four of them. I'd lost track. Five, if we counted the one

Thurston gifted dear old Dad after he forced me to agree to this farce of a marriage.

Transport craft flew overhead, the hum of their electric engines barely noticeable above the chatter of a wide variety of aliens striding down the walkway around me. Some lived here; others were tourists from distant planets.

Oh, to be as free as them, to choose where I wanted to go and who I wanted to marry. To be free to live my own life.

"Jennifer," Thurston bellowed behind me. "Get back here."

"No," I hissed. Never again.

I skittered forward, nearly falling when my stupid heel was sucked down into a crack in the concrete. I yanked it off and smacked it on the stone, breaking off the heel. Then the other.

With my billowy white skirts bunched in my hand, I bolted, my bag jostling against my thigh. I didn't have much inside, just a few changes of clothing and the credits I'd skimmed off the trust my grandmother left me —the one my father controlled, though it should've been handed over to me three years ago when I turned twenty-five.

I had nothing else, not even a solid plan. Get to the transport hub and blend in with the crowd, something I couldn't do until I'd found a place to ditch my floofy white gown. I stood out like the topper on a lush wedding cake.

Everyone pointed, and when cries from my father and Thurston grew louder behind me, those watching melted back against the buildings.

A glance over my shoulder showed they were too close. I cringed, worried I wasn't going to get away.

With fear and desperation charging through my veins, I ran faster. I spiraled around one corner and then another, weaving through the city until their cries grew fainter.

I thought I'd escaped them. Then a soft chitter reached my ears. Shit, they'd sent a tracker. If the mechanical bounty hunter locked onto me, I'd never get away.

I peered around, looking for a place to hide.

A sign hanging from a shop just ahead drew my eye. *Intergalactic Employment Agency.*

I didn't need a job, but they might have a back door I could slink through after using their bathroom to change.

When I slammed inside, a bell overhead jangled. Breathing fast, I turned and peered through the plexi, watching as the tracker soared down the street.

Still looking, then. My breath whooshed from me.

"Come for a job, have you?" a female with a crotchety voice said from behind me. "At the Intergalactic Employment Agency, we're determined to place you in the position of your dreams."

Any job was a dream position if Thurston wasn't part of it.

I turned, plastering a smile on my face. "Hi."

"I have to say, we don't get many brides in here," the gray-haired woman said, her pale blue eyes sparkling as she took in my dress and white shoes with snapped-off heels. Thin and a few inches taller than my five-eight, she wore a polka dot dress with a hem swishing across her knees. "But if you're looking for a job that includes marriage, I'll see what I can do."

"No!" I lowered my voice and tried to control my ragged breathing. "No weddings. I'm not actually here for a—"

Outside, the click of the tracker grew louder. If the droid found me, it would secure my wrists and ankles with unbreakable ties and contain me until my father arrived. Thurston would be hot on Dad's heels, eager to consummate our now-defunct wedding vows.

I stepped closer to the woman and, grabbing her arm, led her to the back of the room where the tracker's beams might not reach.

"I don't have a lot of experience," I said. "But I'm excited to hear about whatever you have to offer that *does not* include marriage."

"All right. We'll leave mail-order brides out of the search." Her rheumy gaze darted to my wrist. "You're not wearing your com."

If I was, the tracker would already have me pinned to the sidewalk. A com held all our data, including past work history. I'd told Thurston I didn't want to wear the clunky device for our wedding, that it would ruin the look I was aiming for. Since I simpered and batted my eyelashes when I said it, he believed me.

"I dropped my com into the dishwater this morning," I said breezily. "I need to get a new one. Tell me about the jobs. I'm looking for something outside the city."

"What about off world?" the woman asked. "I'm Faylene, by the way. I don't normally work this shift, but the regular guy called out sick."

"Off-world jobs?" I asked. "That sounds interesting."

"Let me see what I can find for you." Faylene strolled around behind a counter. A universal com lifted from the surface.

She closed her eyes, accessing the device with the chip implanted within her brain. I'd resisted having mine placed, insisting I preferred using a more antiquated com on my wrist. With an implanted device, I'd never hide from my father or Thurston.

"If you'll allow me to access your data the old-fashioned way," Faylene said, staring at the screen.

A probe extended from my side of the computer, and I laid my thumb on the flat surface for the count of three before pulling it away.

"Jennifer Arasteller," Faylene said, a frown forming on her face. "It doesn't appear you've ever held a job, my dear."

"My father is quite strict about that."

*Women should never work,* he always said. *They should keep busy by caring for their husbands.*

Be controlled, that is.

"I'm a pet whisperer," I said proudly.

Lines appeared on Faylene's brow. "I'm not familiar with that position."

"I can talk animals, creatures, and even beasts into behaving. You've got a hissing pussy cat? I'll make it purr. Even wild dogs eat out of my hand."

Her face cleared. "Ah. Yes. So pet sitting, walking, and care might be job options for you. Let me see." Her eyelids slid closed before popping open. "I have a few off-world positions I can suggest."

"Such as?"

"The Questrians need someone to lead a trail ride into the Veskitan Sector."

Lead a trail ride? Gulp. "What do they ride?"

"Flying kestelars. The trails weave around giant floating islands in the sky."

I didn't mind heights, but . . . "I've never flown on a kestelar before."

"Ah, well. That wouldn't work well for you, then, now would it?" Faylene squinted at the screen. "We also have an opening for an octureet walker in a hootinair."

"What's a hootinair?"

"A harem."

Sounded too close to marriage to Thurston. "Nope."

"When one lacks experience, one can't be picky," Faylene said with a twist of her lips. "However, I have one other position I can offer. A wealthy businessman living on a remote planet has adopted two culair pups and it says here . . ." She leaned closer to the screen. "He's finding them a bit of a challenge."

What was a culair?

A clicking sound erupted behind me, and a glance through the plexi showed the tracker hovering outside the door, its seeking beam skimming back and forth across the floor, coming this way. Damn, it would find me. Would it enter the business or wait for me to emerge? I couldn't stay inside forever.

"You wouldn't happen to have a back door, would you?" I asked. I'd find someplace else to change.

"We do not," she said, her gaze taking in the tracker. "What is a—"

"Awesome," I bellowed, making her jump. "I'll take the job."

Faylene's head tilted, and she frowned at the bag hanging from my arm. "Would you like to go home and pack? I can send a shuttle for you tomorrow."

"I'd like to leave immediately."

"Dressed like that?"

"Wedding dresses are the latest fashion. Everyone's using them for daily wear."

"Why would they do something like that?" Faylene asked, tapping her chin. "I sense something unusual about this transaction."

That was an understatement.

The tracker rammed against the door. My skin jolted, and my heart beat furiously against the lace bodice of my dress.

"I need to leave now," I said, rushing around the counter to grab Faylene's arm. "Please."

She shook her head, making her low bun quiver. "All

right." With a tug away from my grasp, she stepped backward. "I'll call for a shuttle immediately." A pinch of her eyes, and a rumble rang out in the back of the room.

When the pod hit the floor with a thud, the plexi hatch opened.

"I'll notify Vengestire that you'll be arriving," Faylene said.

"Vengestire?"

"Your new employer, Vengestire Rarkeleone Abesteen."

"Thanks." While the tracker banged on the front door, I hurried over to the pod and stepped inside. Talk about a tight escape. "How long will I travel before I arrive?"

"It will take three lunar eclipses of this planet to reach Darkfire. But you'll remain in stasis."

"Darkfire?"

"It's a small planet in the Westula Quadrant. There are only a few residents in the town area, but this is a short-term position, and I doubt you'll have much time to miss bustling city life. You'll be back here before you know it."

If I were lucky, I'd never return to Earth. I had no idea where I'd go after this job finished, but I'd have time to plot a trailless escape. Once I'd found a secure location, I could begin the process of wrestling control of my trust away from my father. "Darkfire sounds lovely."

I dropped my bag by my feet and straps wound around my arms and thighs to hold me in place.

As the pod lid sealed, locking me inside, Faylene waved goodbye and grinned.

I had to wonder what I was getting myself into.

But anything was better than marrying Thurston.

---

You can pick up your copy of *Leashing the Alien* on Amazon.

Printed in Great Britain
by Amazon